COULD ELLRAY BE LOSING A FRIEND?

"Kevin rode his skateboard to school again. With *Jared*," my friend Corey Robinson tells me in a gloomy voice a few minutes before school starts.

"No big deal," I say, trying to shrug like I mean it.

"I guess Kevin forgot about that time Jared tried to beat you up," Corey says. "And it's more like Kevin and Jared are *scooters*, not skaters," he adds, scoffing.

I think Corey is hoping to make us both feel better when he says this.

"It's not like they can actually do any tricks," Corey explains. "They just push themselves down the sidewalk with one foot. Any baby could do that."

I can't. Not yet. "It's still faster than walking," I say, turning away as the buzzer sounds and the rain really starts to fall. Us boys will be steaming in Ms. Sanchez's toasty class with its clanking radiators as our clothes dry, but we don't care.

And I don't care if Kevin has a new friend, I tell myself as Corey and I walk to Ms. Sanchez's class. People make new friends all the time. That doesn't mean *we* aren't still friends.

Does it?

OTHER BOOKS YOU MAY ENJOY

EllRay Jakes Is a Rock Star!	Sally Warner/Jamie Harper
EllRay Jakes Is NOT *a Chicken!*	Sally Warner/Jamie Harper
EllRay Jakes the Dragon Slayer!	Sally Warner/Brian Biggs
EllRay Jakes Walks the Plank!	Sally Warner/Jamie Harper
Friendship According to Humphrey	Betty G. Birney
George Brown, Class Clown: Super Burp!	Nancy Krulik/ Aaron Blecha
George Brown, Class Clown: Trouble Magnet	Nancy Krulik/ Aaron Blecha
Horrible Harry and the Green Slime	Suzy Kline/ Frank Remkiewicz
Horrible Harry Bugs the Three Bears	Suzy Kline/ Frank Remkiewicz
Horrible Harry Goes Cuckoo	Suzy Kline/Amy Wummer
Only Emma	Sally Warner/Jamie Harper
Super Emma	Sally Warner/Jamie Harper
The World According to Humphrey	Betty G. Birney

EllRay Jakes and the Beanstalk

BY **Sally Warner**

ILLUSTRATED BY

Brian Biggs

PUFFIN BOOKS
An Imprint of Penguin Group (USA)

PUFFIN BOOKS
An imprint of Penguin Young Readers Group
Published by the Penguin Group
Penguin Group (USA)
375 Hudson Street
New York, New York 10014, U.S.A.

USA / Canada / UK / Ireland / Australia / New Zealand / India / South Africa / China
Penguin Books Ltd, Registered Offices: 80 Strand, London WC2R 0RL, England

For more information about the Penguin Group visit www.penguin.com

Published simultaneously in the United States of America by Viking Children's Books and
Puffin Books, imprints of Penguin Young Readers Group, 2013

THE LIBRARY OF CONGRESS HAS CATALOGED THE VIKING EDITION AS FOLLOWS:
Warner, Sally, date.
EllRay Jakes and the beanstalk / by Sally Warner ; illustrated by Brian Biggs.
pages cm
Summary: When EllRay's best friend starts hanging out with skateboarders,
EllRay tries to learn how to skateboard to win him back.
ISBN 978-0-670-78499-8 (hardcover)
[1. Friendship—Fiction. 2. Skateboarding—Fiction. 3. African Americans—Fiction.]
I. Biggs, Brian, illustrator. II. Title.
PZ7.W24644Elg 2013 [Fic]—dc23 2012047734

Puffin Books ISBN 978-0-14-242359-2

Printed in the United States of America Book design by Nancy Brennan

10

To Janet Bockus, my Brownie leader—and the last mom—with love and gratitude —S.W.

*

To Liam —B.B.

CONTENTS

★ ★ ★

✲ 1 ✲

KEVIN, COREY, AND ME

"Kevin rode his skateboard to school again. With *Jared*," my friend Corey Robinson tells me in a gloomy voice a few minutes before school starts. It is Friday, and we are standing together on the playground. It is a cold April day, and a few spatters of rain hit our faces.

"No big deal," I say, trying to shrug like I mean it.

Corey's voice sounds funny when he's telling me about Kevin McKinley and Jared Matthews, because Jared has been kind of like our **ENEMY** for two years now. The enemy of Kevin, Corey, and me, I mean, because the three of us are best friends. We are all in the third grade at Oak Glen Primary School.

I've known Kevin since first grade, when my family moved to Oak Glen from San Diego. He showed me how to use the pencil sharpener. I still

remember how the shavings smelled. He and I were—and still are—the only two boys with brown skin in our class, but that's not why we're friends. Well, it's not the *only* reason. The point is, we go "way back," as my dad sometimes says. And things should stay the same.

This is hard to explain, but it's embarrassing to me that Kevin is suddenly so good at skating when I haven't even started learning yet. And I'm secretly hating that he's hanging out with Jared, who has done lots of stuff to embarrass me in the past.

I don't know why Jared does it. Teasing me is kind of like his hobby.

It's not official or anything about Kevin, Corey, and me being **BEST FRIENDS**, by the way. It's not like with the girls in my class, who say, "Heather's my *first* best friend, and Kry's my *second* best friend," as if each girl in my class is keeping her eye on a race that nobody can see. No boy, anyway.

But with us three boys, we just like to hang together, that's all. And some guys are easier to hang with than others. Like I said, Jared can be kind of a pain. His best friend and loyal stooge has always been Stanley Washington, but right now, Jared and *Kevin* are together, putting their skateboards away in the pen in the corner of the playground. I don't see Stanley anywhere.

The pen is where bikes and boards are locked up during the day—since the teachers don't want kids skating out of class when things get dull, I guess.

The rule at Oak Glen is that starting in third grade, you can ride your bike, scooter, or skateboard to school if you wear a helmet. Since my friends and me are in the third grade, this has been a big deal for some of us this year. So far, though, I've only ridden my bike to school four times. But that's because getting up, washing, dressing, eating, then finding my homework, helmet, and bike lock, and still leaving on time for school is too hard for me to pull off.

I'm not that great early in the morning.

And once, when I *did* manage to ride my bike to school, I forgot all about it! I walked home, leaving it locked up and lonely all night long. I got scolded by our school's grouchy custodian, too. You usually only see him when somebody hurls in class and he has to show up with his bucket of sawdust, broom, and dustpan.

That's gotta be one hard job. Corey could never do it. He's so sensitive that he starts to throw up just *thinking* about somebody else doing it. And once, when Fiona McNulty cried in class because someone "looked at her funny," which isn't even a real thing, in my opinion, Corey started crying, too. I also saw him cry at the movies, when a dog died. He had to blow his nose on his sleeve.

Now, when somebody cries in class, which hardly ever happens because Ms. Sanchez is on top of stuff like that, Corey told me he pinches his leg real hard and stares out the window until the other person has mopped up their tears. *Her* tears, usually.

Corey even **YAWNS** when anyone else yawns, but so does everyone, just about. My dad says there is a scientific reason for yawning—something about people cooling their brains. You might think he's making it up, but maybe he isn't. He's a scientist. He teaches geology—that's mostly about rocks—at a college in San Diego.

Corey is a lot nicer than me, I think. Maybe Corey is nicer than Kevin. I'll never have to worry about *him* dumping me as a friend just because I can't do some random thing like ride a skateboard.

"Dude. They do live kind of close to each other," I point out to Corey, watching Kevin and Jared laugh and shove each other as the prickly rain gets its act together and starts to fall a little harder. "And they both have boards. So I guess . . . "

My voice trails off, because I can't think of how to end my sentence.

"I guess Kevin forgot about that time Jared tried to beat you up," Corey says, like he's finishing my sentence for me. "And it's more like Kevin and Jared are *scooters*, not skaters," he adds, scoffing.

I think Corey is hoping to make us both feel

better when he says this—because he is training to be a swimming champion, so his mom and dad don't want him "risking life and limb" on a skateboard, as they put it. And I don't even have a board. Not yet.

My new neighbor Henry has one, though. And he has a friend named Fly who's a *great* skater.

"Huh?" I say, having missed a few words.

"It's not like they can actually do any tricks," Corey explains again. "They just push themselves down the sidewalk with one foot. Any baby could do that."

I can't. Not yet. "It's still faster than walking," I say, turning away as the buzzer sounds and the rain really starts to fall. Us boys will be steaming in Ms. Sanchez's toasty class with its clanking radiators as our clothes dry, but we don't care.

And I don't care if Kevin has a new friend, I tell myself as Corey and I walk to Ms. Sanchez's class. People make new friends all the time. That it doesn't mean *we* aren't still friends.

Does it?

✲ 2 ✲

A WONDERFUL NEW ASSIGNMENT

"Settle down, ladies and gentlemen. No matter how damp you may be, nobody's going to melt," Ms. Sanchez calls out as she prepares to take attendance.

Ms. Sanchez is the prettiest teacher at Oak Glen Primary School. The girls in our class voted about that once. Ms. Sanchez always smells good, too, like those little white flowers that grow on orange trees. She is going to get married someday to a man named Mr. Timberlake, but he's not the famous one from the movies. It's another Mr. Timberlake, one who runs a sports supply store.

The famous Mr. Timberlake lost out, in my opinion.

I don't know what Ms. Sanchez and her Mr. Timberlake are waiting for. How hard can it be to get married? You just say yes or no, and that's it.

The girls in our class all want to be Ms. Sanchez's flower girls when she finally does get married, but good luck with that. It would be like a NASCAR race, with each girl trying to be first in line. They would wreck the wedding.

I take my seat at the same time I'm avoiding looking at Kevin. He's been waving his arms, trying to get my attention—to say hi late, I guess.

Say hi to Jared, Kevin—if he's such a great new friend of yours.

"Settle down," Ms. Sanchez says again, and she starts calling our names.

Stanley Washington is out sick today, it looks like. Ms. Sanchez frowns—but in a pretty way—as she makes this special mark in the attendance book she sometimes calls her "work of art." I accidentally spilled water on it once, but she still likes me.

"We are starting a wonderful new assignment today," she tells us after the usual boring morning announcements have been made. "I got the idea for it when I was reading fables and folk tales last weekend, including some by Hans Christian Andersen and the Brothers Grimm."

"For babies," Jared cough-says into his hand, and a few seats away, Kevin nods.

Cynthia Harbison's hand shoots up into the air. She is like our class's girl version of Jared, only cleaner and smaller. Her first best friend is Heather Patton, who thinks Cynthia is perfect in every way.

I hear Ms. Sanchez sigh, because she has barely gotten started yet. "Yes, Cynthia?" she asks.

Cynthia stands up like she's about to make an important announcement of her own. "But Ms. Sanchez, it's Friday," she says. "And we always start new things on Monday, not Friday."

Heather nods as Cynthia sits back down.

"Well, I want you all to get a head start on the assignment over the weekend," Ms. Sanchez explains.

A couple of boys groan, like now their whole weekend is going to be ruined thinking about *fables*, but some of the girls are looking interested. "I love stories like that," Annie Pat Masterson whispers. She has red hair and sits next to me.

"Me too," her best friend, Emma McGraw, agrees.

"Let's all quiet down," Ms. Sanchez says, by which she means us, not her. "It is not yet time for discussion. First I want to tell you about the assignment."

Some kids get out their pencils and pens so they can take notes, but not me. I may be the shortest kid in our class, boy *or* girl, but I'm a very good rememberer.

"Before we go any further, though," Ms. Sanchez says with a sharp glance in Jared's direction, "I think I should tell you that these stories aren't for babies. Far from it, in fact. Why, I read an old story from Hans Christian Andersen in which a man's head was cut off and buried in a flowerpot!"

"Eww," a chorus of voices says, like they've been rehearsing all morning.

Okay. I can tell Ms. Sanchez didn't mean to scare us, telling us this story. She was just trying to get some of the guys interested. But I think I'll stay away from Hans Christian Andersen from now on, whoever he is. He sounds like he should be rated R.

Heather Patton starts to chew the end of the skinny little braid that usually hangs down one of her cheeks. She is eyeing with alarm the two flowerpots Ms. Sanchez keeps on our windowsill. One has a sprouted avocado pit in it, and the other is growing sweet potato vines. *Supposedly.*

But no, I tell myself. Those pots aren't big enough to hold a human head.

"Reading all those old stories got me thinking about why they still mean something to us today," Ms. Sanchez says, perching on the edge of her desk, one pointy-toed shoe swinging. Fiona McNulty is the best artist in our class, as well as the shyest kid, and she usually keeps a fashion notebook about everything Ms. Sanchez wears. But I think she's too grossed-out about that human head story to get out her notebook and start drawing.

I'm not the best *anything*, except maybe the best loser of friends.

Unless I put up a fight, that is. Maybe I should have waved back at Kevin?

I'M CONFUSED.

"And here's your assignment," our Ms. Sanchez continues, and she goes to the white board and starts writing.

1. This weekend, find a folk tale or fairy tale or fable or old story that you think says something about you, either your past, present, or future.
2. Write it down. Look up more details about your story online, or in books you have at home. Write those details down, too.
3. Think about why this story is special to you.
4. On Monday, we will work together in class, and each of you will add your own personal story to your tale. And later in the week, you will get to illustrate your story!

Fiona looks excited about that last part.

"Let me give you an example," Ms. Sanchez says, returning to her desk. "Let's say I was doing this assignment. I might think, 'Hmm. What about "Sleeping Beauty" as my choice?' Not that I'm so beautiful," she adds with a modest laugh, even though she *is*. Everyone says so. "But I might pick that story," she continues, "because my handsome prince came along, and we're going to get married."

"And have twelve flower girls, and one *best* flower girl," Cynthia Harbison chimes in.

"Now, listen," Ms. Sanchez says, laughing. "I

think we can forget about the wedding and 'Sleeping Beauty' for a while. There are lots of other stories to choose from. If you look at fables, you might choose 'The Boy Who Cried Wolf' or 'The Grasshopper and the Ant.'"

Annie Pat Masterson's hand goes up. "I choose 'The Little Mermaid,'" she says after Ms. Sanchez has called on her. "Because she's part fish, and fish are my special thing."

She wants to be a fish scientist when she grows up. Whatever that is.

"But mermaids are *my* thing," Heather says, clouding up. "They're even on my sheets."

"More than one person can use the same story," Ms. Sanchez assures us. "I promise you that each paper will be unique by the time you've finished with it, even if you all choose 'The Little Mermaid.'"

"Unique" means one-of-a-kind. My dad told me that once. But *I'm* not choosing "The Little Mermaid," who ended up turning into sea foam, if I remember right.

Alfie made my mom come up with a different ending.

"EllRay can be an elf," Jared calls out.

"We'll have none of that," Ms. Sanchez warns him. "Or I'll start assigning stories *to* you. And I can think of some **DOOZIES**, believe me."

We do believe her. Ms. Sanchez does not mess around when it comes to keeping her class in order.

Of course, the playground is another matter—and it's almost time for nutrition break.

3

WHO ARE YOU GOING TO BE?

"Who are you going to be?" Corey asks me as we grab our snacks—excuse me, *nutrition*—from our backpacks and hurry outside. It has stopped raining, but the playground looks black and shiny. Drops of rain are still clinging to the chain-link fence, making it sparkle.

"I don't know yet," I say, trying to see where Kevin is. Maybe he'll hang with us like nothing ever happened.

Maybe nothing *did* happen. Maybe Kevin and Jared just came to school on their boards at the same time.

"I think I'm going to be 'The Tortoise and the Hare,'" Corey says, peeling off a strip of string cheese and popping it into his mouth. String cheese and almonds are his favorite snack.

"Which one?" I ask. "The tortoise or the hare?"

"Both," Corey says, smiling. "I'm the tortoise when I have to stand in front of the class and do something, and I'm the hare when I'm swimming. Because I'm really **FAST**."

"I'm not sure that's the moral of the story," I tell him, trying to remember.

"What's a moral? I forget."

"It's the lesson the story is trying to teach," I say. "At least when it's a fable. My mom reads this old book to us sometimes before we go to sleep."

"Huh," Corey says, peeling off some more cheese.

Annie Pat and Emma appear, dipping their hands into their snack bags like birds pecking at seeds. "I think Emma should be Thumbelina," Annie Pat says, smiling. "Because she's such a tiny little thing."

"I *might* be Thumbelina," Emma says, thinking it over. "I'll have to look her up first, in case she doesn't have a happy ending."

"Well, I'm going to be Cinderella," Cynthia announces, smoothing her hair back with her red plastic headband. "Both our names sound like they start the exact same way. And Heather can be one of my stepsisters. And maybe Fiona can be the mouse who helps me clean up the kitchen."

"One of the *ugly* stepsisters?" Heather asks, her mouth stopping mid-chew.

It looks like Heather might stand up to Cynthia at last!

"You don't have to be *that* ugly," Cynthia assures her. "Just a little, maybe."

"I'm not sure I want to be a mouse," Fiona almost squeaks, which basically ruins her objection. All that's missing is whiskers and a tail.

"And anyway," Kry Rodriguez points out to Cynthia in a friendly way, "I don't think the idea is for you to tell other kids what they have to be. It's not like they're all characters in a play about you."

"It was just an idea," Cynthia says, her nose in the air. But she doesn't ever fight with Kry, because everybody likes her. I don't know how Kry does that.

"Well, *my* idea was to be the Little Match Girl," Fiona dares to say. "Because she was really shivery and cold, like I am now," she explains. "And she saw a shooting star once, and I did, too. And she probably had weak ankles, just like me."

Nobody seems to know what to do with all this information coming out of Fiona's mouth. She hardly ever says a word!

"What about you?" Kry finally asks Jared.

"Maybe the Pied Piper," Jared says, shrugging. "And you guys can follow me wherever I go."

Yeah, right. *That's* gonna happen.

"Stanley's not here today," Jared continues. "But he can be the grasshopper from 'The Grasshopper and the Ant.' I'll tell him."

"I'm not sure the grasshopper is the hero of that story," Kry reminds him.

"Maybe not," Jared says. "But he has all the fun."

"I think I'll be Snow White," Heather says almost to herself. "I do like to sleep a lot."

"Or you could be Rapunzel," Cynthia says. "Because you have such long, beautiful hair."

Heather cheers up, hearing this. A compliment from Cynthia is like an endangered species, it's so rare. And I can tell for sure that Heather likes the idea of being Rapunzel a whole lot better than being an ugly stepsister. Maybe even more than being Snow White.

"What about you?" Emma asks Kry.

"Hmm," Kry says, tapping her chin. "I'm thinking either Little Red Riding Hood, because I love to visit my *abuela*, and we always bring her cookies. Or I'll be Tinkerbell, if that even counts as a story. I'd like to make people's wishes come true."

"EllRay can be the Ugly Duckling if he's not gonna be an elf, right?" Jared says, poking Kevin in the ribs with his elbow. "Or Pinocchio, because he lies like a rug."

"I do not lie," I say, defending myself—since it doesn't look like Kevin's going to do it for me. "Maybe I'll be Jack, from 'Jack and the Beanstalk.' He ended up climbing the beanstalk and killing the giant, don't forget."

"Yeah," Cynthia says. "After he sold his mom's whole entire cow for some magic beans."

"It ended up good, though," I say, but I can feel my face get hot. I'd forgotten about those beans.

I still like the idea of "Jack and the Beanstalk,"

though. He climbed up that beanstalk one great big leaf at a time, didn't he? Even though he didn't know what he'd find when he got to the top? Jack was **BRAVE**.

And I'm the one who gets to decide.

THAT FEELING

"Finally," Kevin says during our last recess. He has managed to corner me near the playground drinking fountain, where the water tastes so weird that you only drink it if you're dying of thirst.

"Finally what?" I say, like I don't know what he's talking about.

As if I didn't spend lunch in the library instead of the cafeteria, where all the action is on cold, wet days.

"What's the matter?" Kevin asks. "Are you avoiding me? Do I stink or something?" he says, sniffing his parka-covered armpits in a jokey way.

"Nah. You smell okay, I guess," I say, shoving my hands into my jacket pockets. "I've been busy today, that's all."

I can't think of a way to joke back at him.

"Busy with what?" Kevin asks, like he's really

curious. "Dude, it's Oak Glen. There's nothing to do here but hang with each other. And Corey had to leave school early for a swim meet."

See, that's the trouble with having Corey as one of your best friends. He has an actual schedule, like a grown-up. So he's not always around.

"You've been busy with what?" Kevin asks again.

"I dunno," I say.

I can't really tell him the truth, that I'm jealous he rode his skateboard to school with Jared this morning. That would sound so—so *girly*. Like, *"Ooh, I'm so jealous."*

And I'm not *jealous*-jealous. I mean, sure, Kevin and I have always been friends. And there's nothing wrong with him making another friend. What do I care? "The more the merrier," like my mom sometimes says.

But why did Kevin have to choose *Jared Matthews* if he needed a new friend? Jared and his buddy Stanley are like a two-person team whose mission is to make me look bad—in front of as many people as possible.

The more the merrier.

"You should learn to skate," Kevin tells me, and

then he clears his throat, which means he's getting ready to say something important. I know him, see?

"Skating is so cool," he begins. "Even when it's raining, like today, you can just pick up your board and take it with you anywhere. Into your mom's car, or into the mall. Even into the movies, if they let you. Having a skateboard is like being a teenager and being able to *drive*, EllRay."

Kevin exaggerates like that sometimes.

"When did you get to be such an expert?" I ask, staring hard at the pavement.

"I'm not," he protests. "I can't even ollie yet, and I don't think Jared can, either. But my older cousin skates, and I was at his house a lot during winter break. Remember those days I couldn't come over? Anyway, he gave me one of his old boards and made me keep practicing on my own. It's hard," he admits.

Kevin likes solving puzzles and stuff. I guess learning to skate is sort of like a puzzle for him.

"You never said," I tell him, trying to keep the blame out of my voice.

"But it wasn't a *secret*," Kevin says, looking confused. "There's a lot of things I don't say. Like, I brushed my teeth after breakfast," he tells me, trying for another joke. "I never told you that, either, did I? But I will from now on, if you want me to."

"That's okay," I say, trying to joke back. "Maybe you did tell me, and I just wasn't listening. So, you practice all the time with Jared, now?" I slip in this question like it's nothing. No big deal, just something to say.

"Not *all* the time," Kevin says. "Just a couple

of times. Like when he wanted me to come to the park last weekend. He's not so bad when he's on his own."

"Huh," I say, trying to think fast how to reply, which always works the opposite for me. The faster I try to think, the **SLOWER** my brain goes.

Okay. I'm not the boss of Kevin, I remind myself. He can hang out with whoever he wants. Also, he's right—Jared's *not* so bad when he's on his own. It's Jared-and-Stanley that becomes the awful mix.

Maybe I'll just do whatever it takes to stay friends with Kevin. I can ignore Jared if I have to.

"You should learn," Kevin is saying again, smiling at me like today has been perfectly normal. "It's really fun, EllRay. And if you learned, we could all—"

"Maybe," I interrupt. "I *might* learn. I'll think about it."

But it won't be with Kevin and Jared, I promise myself.

No. I'm counting on my neighbor Henry's friend Fly to teach me, even though I'm not sure Fly likes me that much.

See, my plan now is to surprise Kevin with how

good a skater I am, once I learn. Then Kevin will remember that he's *glad* we're friends. Maybe then he won't need to hang around with Jared anymore.

Then things will go back to the way they used to be.

Skating does have one thing going for it, I remind myself. The kids who ride their boards to school act like they have a secret nobody else knows: that freedom is there, waiting for them in the playground pen.

It's the same way Jack must have felt, sneaking out of his hut to climb the beanstalk. *Sure*, his mom was mad at him for selling their only cow. *Sure*, Jack didn't know what he'd find at the top of the beanstalk. But he climbed it anyway. Didn't he?

So, not only do I want my old friend Kevin back, *I want that feeling.*

And I'm gonna get it!

5

HENRY SAYS

"Can I use your shaggy rug?" I ask Alfie, my four-year-old sister. She is very cute, but please don't tell her that. She's bad enough.

It is now Sunday afternoon, two days after my awkward talk with Kevin, and I am standing in the hall outside Alfie's pink and purple bedroom. My new skateboard is tucked under my arm. I am trying to pretend that carrying it around is a normal thing, like how my dad carries his briefcase. But it still feels weird. And heavy.

"What do you want my rug for?" Alfie asks. She is lying on her puffy bedspread, with a few plastic horses lined up in front of her. The horses are very un-horsey colors—orange, purple, blue. They also have long, silky manes and tails they would trip on in real life.

Alfie is not big on real life, though, so that's okay.

"Henry says that first, I'm supposed to practice just standing on my board," I say, wishing I didn't have to explain this to Alfie. But maybe having to do stuff you don't want to is part of reaching a goal. Alfie's rug is almost like grass, it's so thick—and I'm not about to practice on the front lawn where anyone could see me.

Especially Henry and Fly, in case Fly calls me a **POSER**, which is what older guys call skaters they don't like. Ones who don't know what they're doing. Or in case I fall off.

Henry Pendleton is ten years old, and like I said, he is my very cool new neighbor. It will be hard living up to him. And Fly Reilly is Henry's eleven-year-old best friend—his best skating friend, anyway. Henry says you should hang with kids who are better than you at what you're trying to do.

That shouldn't be hard for *me*. So far, all I'm good at is holding my new board under my arm.

It isn't really new, by the way. Me and my dad found it for eight dollars at a yard sale yesterday. Yard sales are one of the things we like to do together on Saturday afternoons. Dad said buying a used board was the ecological and thrifty thing to do. He said that he and mom would get me a good one in a few months—if I learned to ride and be safe at the same time, and if I was still interested in skating then.

That's a whole lot of "ifs."

Of course, me bringing home even a bashed-up, eight-dollar used skateboard meant that my mom started to look up special shoes, helmets, and pads on the Internet almost the second we walked through the door. After her first freak-out, I mean. Dad said he's not sure how economical this whole skating thing is turning out to be after all.

"You can't *take* my rug," Alfie says, sitting up on her bed like she's about to defend her room against me, the alien invader.

"I want to put my board on it and just stand there," I tell her. "I won't hurt anything. I won't even talk to you," I add, hoping she'll take the hint and not flood me with a lot of babble about unicorns and fairies, or her friends and enemies at Kreative Learning and Playtime Daycare.

And yes, I know they spelled "creative" wrong. Dad mentions that a lot.

"Okay. You can stand on my rug for a nickel," Alfie says, and this doesn't surprise me a bit. Alfie has just started learning about money, and she has decided she wants a lot of it, so I've come prepared. I fish a nickel out of my pocket and put it in her hot little hand.

I take my board and **PLONK** it down in the middle of her rug, then I climb on. I try to copy the way I've seen other guys stand, but it doesn't feel right.

"Which foot goes in front?" Alfie asks, tilting her head. "Can we vote?"

See, they voted on what to name the hamster at Kreative Learning, so that's another big thing for Alfie now. I think "Hammy" won, by the way.

"No voting," I inform her. "You can do it 'regular foot' or '**GOOFY FOOT**,' Henry says. There's no right or wrong. It's whichever seems more natural," I add, even though nothing is seeming very natural to me right now.

After all, I am standing on a skateboard on the shaggy pink rug in my little sister's room. What's so natural about that?

"'*Henry says*,'" Alfie repeats, quoting me. "I thought that was his name when he first moved in, you said it so much."

"Did not," I argue, even though she's probably right.

"So, just put one foot in front, and push with the other one," Alfie says. She can be kind of bossy sometimes.

"Wait," I tell her. "Henry says there's a way to find out which foot pushes."

"What's the way?"

"I just stand here with my feet on the rug, see,"

I say, getting off the board, "and you sneak up behind me and try to knock me over."

"It's not sneaking if you already know I'm coming," Alfie points out, but she's off the bed and ready to tackle me before I can even count to one.

"Wait," I say again, holding up my hand like it's a stop sign. "Go behind me and *then* push."

"With no warning?"

"With no warning," I say.

And so Alfie strolls around behind me like she just happens to be going for a walk around her room. "La-di-da-di-dah," she sings, and then **WHAM**, I'm staggering forward—*right foot first.*

"Good job, Alfie," I say, before she can shove me again. "So that's my rear kicking foot, and my left foot will be up front, for balancing. I'm regular foot."

"Too bad," Alfie says, like I just lost a prize. "But so far, all you're doing is talking. I'll bet I could stand on your board without anyone even pushing me first. Give me a turn, EllWay. Please?"

"EllWay" is Alfie-speak for EllRay. That's just the way she says my name.

"You can have a turn after me, maybe," I say,

getting on the board and taking my stance: left foot forward, over the front wheels, and right foot back, as if it's ready to push. I bend my knees like I'm zooming along, arms out.

"Are you pretending you're an *airplane*?" Alfie asks, her brown eyes wide.

"Nuh-uh," I say, still racing down the street—in my head, anyway—as I try to remember everything Henry said about this first lesson. I shift my weight toward the front wheels, then back toward the rear wheels. And then I try to jump a little.

"You're wrecking my rug," Alfie objects, watching me. "That's gonna cost you more. I'm saving up for a Golden Sparkle Corral for my horsies," she tells me, as if I didn't already know. Everyone knows.

"I can't go downstairs and do this," I say. "Mom would probably make me wear a helmet—*indoors*. And that would ruin the whole effect."

"Yeah," loyal Alfie agrees. "It would wreck everything. *Mom*," she adds, sounding scornful and guilty at the same time, because usually, she's a big fan of our mom. "You must be the best skater in your whole class, EllWay," she adds as I sway from side to side.

"Not even close," I admit. "But maybe someday. So far, Kevin McKinley is best, if you can believe it. And after him comes Jared Matthews. And then Kry Rodriguez, if you count the girls. But Henry Pendleton is going to be my secret weapon, because he knows Fly."

"I could skate as good as Kry if I wanted to," Alfie brags, basing this statement on absolutely nothing. "You *said* I could have a turn, EllWay. Let me try! But push me over first, okay? So I can see what foot I am? I hope I'm goofy foot."

"I'm sure you are," I say, getting off my board. "But I'm *not* going to push you. That would be the exact minute Dad walks into the room, and you know it. Go ahead and try, though."

Alfie grabs my hand and climbs onto the board, which probably can't tell anything is on it at all. Even though I am small, Alfie is tinier. Her real name is "Alfleta," and that means "beautiful elf" in this ancient language only our mom knows about. And Alfie *is* like a golden-brown elf, now that I think about it.

“How’s this?” Alfie says, still gripping my hand.

“Good,” I tell her. “But please don’t fall off, or I’ll never hear the end of it.”

“When do we get to start *moving*?” Alfie asks, scowling.

“We have to learn this first,” I say. “At least that’s what—”

“*Henry says*,” Alfie finishes, crouching over my new-old skateboard like she really knows what she’s doing.

Which she absolutely does *not*.

✲ 6 ✲

STANDING UP TO JARED

"Hey, loser," Jared calls out to me on the playground on Monday morning before school, even though you're not allowed to call anyone that at Oak Glen. But what does Jared care? He's like a third grade giant! "Did you ride your tricycle to school today, or did your *Mommy* drive you again?"

"Shut up," I tell him, which you are also not supposed to say.

We have a lot of rules at our school, but no grown-ups are around.

We don't have any official bullies in our class, not the kind on TV shows, but Jared is the boy who sometimes comes closest to being one. And like I already said, Cynthia Harbison is the girl version of him. Next in the mean line for the boys comes Stanley Washington, Jared's friend, who is back in school today. I wonder if he obeyed Jared's command and decided to be the grasshopper, from "The Grasshopper and the Ant"?

"Loser," Jared jeers again. "If we ever have a skating contest, you can be in charge of watching."

"Yeah," Stanley chimes in right after stuffing some orange tortilla chips into his mouth. I guess he's feeling better.

He's been keeping a close eye on Kevin and Jared, I can tell.

Maybe Kevin and Jared's new friendship is as weird for Stanley as it is for me.

"Yuck," Cynthia says, skipping by arm-in-arm with Heather on their way to the chain-link fence, where they like to hang out. And sometimes they just *hang*, a few inches off the ground. "Keep your mouth shut when you chew, Stanley Washington. Don't you know anything?"

Cynthia thinks she is the big expert on manners around here.

Jared would probably say something back, but I think he kind of likes Heather. A little, anyway. He blushes whenever he talks to her.

"If we ever *do* have a skating contest," I tell Jared after Cynthia and Heather have skipped away, "you'd better know how to do more than just push your board down the sidewalk. That's not skating, that's scooting," I add, repeating Corey's put-down of how far Jared and Kevin have gotten with their skating skills.

Of course, I still can't even **SCOOT** yet.

Jared's cheeks are getting red, and his twirly, sticking-up hair seems to bristle with rage.

"Shut up," Stanley tells me.

That's the same thing I just said to Jared, which proves that what Ms. Sanchez claims is true: that saying bad words can be contagious, like the flu.

"You shut up," I say to Stanley. "I have a board, you know. So maybe we *should* have a scooting—I mean *skating*—contest," I add, turning back to Jared. "That way you and Kevin could show all the kids how great you are."

"And me too. I'm learning, too," Stanley pipes up, his hair flopping over his glasses. "I'm already way better than Kevin."

"We'd do it in a second," Jared tells me, his chin up. "Only we're not allowed to skate at school. In case you forgot."

"There's always the park," I remind him.

The Eustace B. Pennypacker Memorial Park is the park nearest our school. It's where Jared and I had our so-called fight that time.

"Mmm. Maybe," Jared says, like he's trying to figure out if the the park is challenging enough for all the advanced tricks he, Kevin, and Stanley can land. "I'll look at it."

"He'll look at it," Stanley echoes.

"Go away, grasshopper," I tell him just as the buzzer sounds.

"Hey," Stanley says, scowling. "How did you know about that?"

"I'm a real good guesser," I say over my shoulder as we head for class.

"Loser," Jared calls after me, but I'm barely even listening anymore.

Standing up to Jared—even a little—feels good, like I'm getting closer to my goal.

✲ 7 ✲

HENRY AND FLY

It's Tuesday afternoon, and I'm not any better at skating now than I was on Sunday.

"Little *dude*. Over here," Fly Reilly calls out in his bossy way from the big turnaround area at the back of Henry's driveway. Henry and Fly are going to build a plywood ramp and something they call a grind box there some day. Maybe they'll even let me help, Henry said. But plywood costs a lot of money, it turns out, so I'm not holding my breath.

How much stuff costs is a total mystery to me. I can see how a decorated birthday cake might cost a lot of money, because everyone loves birthday cake, and it's hard to make those frosting roses. My mom tried to learn once, and we got to eat the mistakes—for a while, anyway.

But *plywood* costing a lot of money? It's all over the place!

I don't know what Fly's real first name is, and it's not like I'm about to ask. But Henry told me in private that Fly got his nickname when he was four, because his aunties thought he was so cute. **"SO FLY."** Personally, I don't see it. When I first met Fly, I thought he was called that because he's always moving around. It's like he thinks someone might be spying on him from the bushes, and he'd better keep moving, *or else*.

"Hey, EllRay," Henry says in his usual friendly way, and he gives me a grin.

Henry Pendleton is tall and super-skinny, "all arms and legs," my mom says when she talks about him.

"With some banged-up knees and elbows thrown in," my dad usually adds, shaking his head.

And that's not even mentioning the road rash and bruises Henry wears on his body like they are badges of honor.

Alfie acts even girlier than usual around Henry, so I try to keep her away from him, and definitely away from Fly. Fly doesn't have any little brothers or sisters, so he has zero tolerance. Alfie can be kind of a pest, I'm the first to admit, and sometimes

I get the feeling Henry and Fly are barely tolerating *me*. Fly, anyway.

"You been practicing your stance?" Fly asks me, scowling, one foot jiggling up and down on his board. He looks like a spider about to scoot across its web to devour some dumb mosquito that got trapped in it. *Me.*

"Yeah, I practiced," I say. "Inside. On a rug," I admit, saying this almost against my will. But there's no point trying to pull anything over on Fly, I remind myself. He's already got the stink-eye aimed at me—probably because he's got nothing to gain having me hang around him and Henry. What's Fly gonna learn from me? How to land a kickflip or something? Yeah, right.

Fly can already do a five-o grind better than anyone I've ever seen outside of YouTube. He showed me a video on his phone of him doing it from this time he was skating at another kid's house. A kid who has a grind box.

At least I *think* it was Fly on that video. You couldn't really tell, the picture was so small.

Henry kind of *has* to invite me over every so often, even though he's ten and I'm eight. We're

next-door neighbors. We even played Battleship once when it rained. That game's hard! And I hadn't played an actual board game since I was Alfie's age and Dad used to beat me at checkers, trying to teach me to be a good sport—which is something I'm still working on, by the way.

Meaning—I hate to lose.

Anyway, Henry won the game, and I somehow managed to hide my clenchy fists and the sparks coming out of my ears long enough to say, "Good job, Henry. Congratulations."

But I'm nothing but a pain to Fly, who is eleven years old, remember. He's got three years on me.

That's almost the same difference as between me and Alfie!

Fly is in between me and Henry when it comes to tallness, like I said, but he's a lot fussier than either one of us about his hair, his clothes, his shoes. His everything. I guess having to go to all that trouble when you get dressed is the price you pay for looking so good.

"Practice some more," Fly commands me. "Right here on the driveway, on your board. Not on a rug. If you fall, you fall. So be it." And he flops onto the little patch of lawn next to the Pendletons' turnaround.

"Or just practice pushing and turning," Henry suggests, like he can tell I don't want to stand there on my board in front of Fly. He probably knows I'm afraid the board will turn against me, and I'll end up planted facedown on the driveway.

No doubt Fly would get *that* on his phone, too, and I'd be a joke all over the world in about six minutes flat. He'd probably add some funny music while he was at it!

WHUH, WHUH.

Thanks, Internet.

"I get the pushing part, but how do you make the board turn?" I ask.

"You kind of *lean.* It's hard to explain," Henry says, getting back to work on his ollie, which is the most basic skating trick there is. It's how you get your board in the air so you can do stuff. But it's harder than it looks, and for some kids it can take like a year, even if they're usually pretty coordinated—like Henry. Fly is tutoring him, and this is what he says about doing an ollie:

1. First you crouch, with your feet in a wide V shape.
2. Your back foot is *way* back, and your front foot is over the front wheels.
3. Then you push down on your back foot to make the whole board jump into the air.
4. When you're in the air, you slide your front foot forward to level the board.
5. Then you land with your knees bent.
6. And your feet stay glued to the board the whole time.

It's hard to explain, but ollies are important. All other skate tricks are based on them.

For example, even though you can skate *off* a

curb onto the street without knowing how to do one, you need an ollie to jump your board up onto the next curb.

"Did you bring any food, kid?" Fly asks me as I take my stance on my board and cautiously push off with my right foot. I pretend-cross my fingers for luck, since I'm afraid to cross them for real. One more thing to remember and I'll topple over for sure.

"Nuh-uh," I say, jumping off the board, because I don't know how to stop it yet. Food? I was supposed to bring food?

"Well, we're hungry," Fly informs me. "And if you wanna hang with us, you gotta pay—with food, 'cause that's all you got going for you. That's the rule. It's not like we're *babysitters*. Which reminds me, tell your little sister to stop peeking at us."

"She peeks at you?" I say.

"Yeah," Fly says, scowling. "From your upstairs window, and sometimes through the fence. She gets on my nerves."

"Alfie's not so bad," Henry objects, his voice mild. "And EllRay doesn't have to bring any food." His feet are making the required wide V shape, and his right foot is way toward the back of his board, like Fly said.

"Bend your knees more," Fly says from the lawn, barely looking at him. "Kind of *crouch* before you make the board jump. But I'm hungry," he says to me, like that's the second part of his sentence. "And Henry told me your mom makes really good snacks."

"I could bring food next time, I guess," I say, like it's this great idea that just popped into my very own head.

"Only if you want to," Henry tells me, crouching as directed. And *down* comes the weight of his back foot at the very end of his board, and *up* goes the nose.

And down goes Henry.

"Dude, slide!" Fly shouts. "You didn't slide your front foot forward fast enough to level the board in the air. And you're supposed to land with your knees bent, too. Not *on* your knees."

And he jumps up and does a couple of perfect ollies like they're nothing at all.

"Do it again," Fly tells Henry, his hands on his hips.

And, to me, "Food. Next time. And it better be good, *little dude*."

I shrug—like maybe I'll bring food, and maybe I won't.

But I will.

"And do something about your stupid little sister," Fly adds, scowling.

"She's not stupid. But I'll talk to her," I say, hating the words even as I say them.

They make me feel like I'm slipping backward.

I start pushing with my right foot again, mostly just trying to stay on the board—and to keep Fly from yelling at me.

I'll try turning tomorrow.

Alone.

✲ 8 ✲

CIVILIZED CONVERSATION

"Dinner's ready. Wash up, you two," Mom calls up the stairs at six o'clock sharp, because that's when we always eat. Dad has been home for about half an hour.

My father's complete name is Dr. Warren Jakes, and he is a big, strong man who wears glasses. He is also very smart. Unfortunately, I do not resemble him in any way—**BIG**, **STRONG**, or **SMART**—except that we both like meat, and plenty of it.

When my dad is away from home, doing research about rocks or something, we eat weird things like eggplant lasagna and stir-fried tofu and vegetables. And pretend cheese, which is just wrong. Cheese should be cheese, or you should just skip it.

No wonder I'm such a pipsqueak, which is what Jared called me one time.

Dad promises I will grow taller, but I am beginning to have my doubts about that.

As we wash our hands, Alfie and I have our usual shoving match at the sink in the bathroom we supposedly share, even though her bottles of shampoo and bubble bath are starting to crowd me out. I'm afraid I will use something of hers by accident in the shower one morning and go to school smelling like flowers or pineapples and mangos.

Like I could live *that* down.

Do something about your stupid little sister, Fly said about an hour ago, talking about Alfie. What's his problem? She's only four!

"I won," Alfie says, a big smile on her face, as she wipes her little starfish hands on her ruffly skirt.

"You can't 'win' washing hands," I inform her.

"But I came in first, EllWay," she says. "And that's the same as winning."

"Let's just go eat," I say, and she sprints off down the hall—so she can be the winner going down the stairs before me, I guess.

Congratulations, Alfie.

★ ★ ★

Our family has this thing my mom and dad call "civilized conversation" when we eat dinner, and here are the rules:

1. Taking turns, each of us says the best thing and the worst thing that happened that day. And no interruptions are allowed.
2. You have to listen to what everyone says, too, not just sit there planning what you are going to say when it's your turn. And there might be a quiz during dessert, so you have to pay attention.
3. Also, you can't argue about someone else's best and worst thing. Like, you can't say, "I don't call *not* getting your hair pulled by Suzette Monahan a good thing, Alfie," or, "Ha! You think *that's* bad? Wait until you hear what happened to me!" It's sharing, not a contest.

"And what was your worst thing today, Louise?" my dad asks my mom, after she has finished telling us her best thing, that she found the perfect girl's name for her new fantasy book. It's Aisley, which means "dwells at the ash tree meadow" in old Saxon, which I think only my mom understands anymore. That'll be on Dad's quiz tonight for sure, if there is one.

My mom writes fantasy books for grown-ups, which is why Alfie and I have such weird names. My real name is Lancelot Raymond, which fortunately got shortened to L-period-Ray when I was little. And that got shortened to EllRay.

Where was my dad when all this goofy baby-naming was going on? Didn't he get a vote?

"My worst thing was dropping the spaghetti box when I got it out of the cupboard," Mom tells us, making a funny face. "It was like pick-up sticks times one hundred. And now it's Miss Alfie's turn," she says, turning to Alfie, who has made a hand puppet out of her napkin and is snapping at me with it under the table.

Calling Alfie "Miss Alfie" is my mom's way of reminding my little sister to be polite, I think.

"Okay, me," Alfie says. "My best thing was when Henry-next-door said I wasn't so bad," she reports, a sunny smile spreading across her round face as she remembers this fabulous moment in history.

"So you *were* spying on us," I say, scowling. "Fly was right! He said you're always peeking through the fence."

"Fly Reilly was at the Pendletons' house again this afternoon?" my dad asks, matching my scowl. My dad likes just about everyone, as much as he even notices them, anyway, but I can tell he's not all that happy about Fly. He doesn't like me hanging out with him, that's for sure. He says it's because Fly's too old for me, but I think it's more than that.

Good thing Dad doesn't know what Fly said about Alfie! He'd probably never let me go over to Henry's again, in case Fly was there.

And I'd *never* learn to skate. I'd be a poser forever.

I mean, I don't like Fly either, not after he complained about Alfie. But you don't have to like someone to learn from them, do you?

And Henry's really cool, and Henry likes Fly. So how bad could Fly be?

"EllRay?" my dad says, reminding me that he asked me a question.

"I didn't know he was going to be there," I say. "And Alfie shouldn't—"

"It's *still my turn* for best and worst," Alfie interrupts, furious. "Just because I'm little doesn't mean you get to talk all over me!"

"Alfie's right," Mom says in her most soothing voice. "What was your worst thing, honey?"

"When everybody talked all over me at dinner," Alfie says, her arms folded across her chest. "My very own family."

"I'm sorry, Alfie," my dad tells her. "It won't happen again. Everyone deserves to be heard."

"Especially me," Alfie says, lifting her chin.

"But EllRay," Dad adds, turning to me, "I think we need to continue our conversation about who you're spending time with. We have to establish some ground rules, son."

"After dinner, maybe?" my mom says, passing the salad for the second time. Alfie peers suspiciously into the bowl for anything that's not lettuce, then helps herself to a couple of sprigs of green.

Mom has a way of suggesting things that's really more like saying, "Look, this is how it's going to be," at least at the dinner table. And my dad always agrees with her.

They're a team.

"After dinner," Dad agrees, helping himself to more salad. "But *right* after dinner son. In my office."

UH-OH. Dad's office!

Not good.

THIS DUMB NEW RULE

"But Henry's our neighbor," I say to my dad for the third time, about ten minutes later. "And he's the only kid anywhere near my age on our whole street, so who else am I supposed to play with? You're always telling me I should make more friends."

Which I had better start doing if I'm losing Kevin, I think, frowning.

That would just leave Corey, and he's usually at swimming practice.

"There's nothing wrong with Henry," Dad tells me from across his shiny wood desk. "And the Pendletons are very good neighbors. We're lucky that house isn't empty anymore."

"So it's okay if I hang with *him*," I say.

"It's fine, as long as at least one parent is home and you ask Mom," Dad says.

"But it's not fine when Fly's there?" I ask, trying to understand this dumb new rule. "Why?"

Dad looks as if he's arguing with himself about whether or not to tell me something. "Fly is three years older than you, EllRay," he begins. "That's one big issue. But let's just say he's been in more than a few scrapes lately. He hasn't been making very good choices."

"Huh," I say.

"Look. The Pendletons know his mother," Dad continues. "And they've been trying to help out by having Fly over after school every so often—to give his afternoons some structure. And that's their decision. But your mother and I don't want you going over to the Pendletons' house when Fly is there. That's *our* decision."

"But—how do you know all that stuff about Fly's scrapes and bad choices?" I ask, trying to make it sound like a regular question, not an argument. "You never even met him! And it's not like he's going to infect me with his badness. You shouldn't punish me because Fly Reilly messed up a couple of times."

"I did meet him once," Dad reminds me. "In the Pendletons' driveway. He wouldn't even look me in the eye or say hello. And he has messed up more than a couple of times, son. Believe me. He's a troubled kid."

"But lots of kids are shy around grown-ups," I point out. "And that doesn't mean he's some gangster, Dad. Just because he didn't look you in the eye."

The idea of a shy Fly almost makes me laugh. He's like the **OPPOSITE** of shy.

But he's also a really good skater, and he's the kid I can learn from.

I can't really explain to Dad about Kevin sort of *skating away* from being one of my two best friends at Oak Glen, and, worse, hanging out now with Jared, my sometimes enemy. Dad would probably call Kevin's father to "talk it through," as he puts it, because they play golf together. And how embarrassing would that be?

Very.

And it would only make things worse between Kevin and me.

"I had a word with Henry's dad about Fly, son,"

Dad says after a really long pause. "That's how I know these things about him. Your mother and I were getting a little concerned, and the subject just happened to come up."

That sounds pretty lame to me. "You say we should never listen to gossip, Dad," I remind him, thinking this is a pretty good point. "And this sounds like gossip to me. Or like Mr. Pendleton tattled about something private."

"Things are different when it's a matter of protecting your own children, son," Dad says. "It's our job to protect *you*."

And it's my job to protect Alfie, I remind myself. But I can handle that.

"So what am I supposed to do?" I ask my dad. "Never go over to Henry's house again? Like you said, it's their choice who they invite over. I can't say, 'Sorry, Pendletons, but no more Fly.' They've already decided about that, which means no more *me*."

"You could call first, to see if Fly is there," Dad suggests, after thinking it over for what seems like a small part of one second.

"Like I'm a *baby*?" I ask, feeling my face getting hot. "Like it's some playdate? We're just hanging, Dad! That's what guys *do.* They don't call first, or wait for some fancy invitation with glitter on it. I mean, I could see calling if Henry lived really far away, just to see if he was home, but he's our *next-door neighbor.* Isn't it bad enough that I'm only eight, and Henry's ten? I'm lucky he lets me come over there at all!"

"Take it or leave it, son," Dad says, already thinking about something else. A rock, probably.

"But—but what if I'm over there with Henry, and Fly just kind of shows up?" I ask, picturing it. "What am I supposed to do then? Go running home like a *girl*?"

"Let's not make any sweeping statements about girls, son," Dad says, actually laughing a little. "And you don't have to *run* home. You can stroll. Or amble. Or mosey. But yes, given that situation, you should come on home."

"Huh," I say, staring down at my bony knees.

At my bony *little* knees. I feel like I'm about three years old.

But—maybe Dad has accidentally given me a way to wriggle out of this terrible new rule. I could always say Fly *just happened* to show up at the last minute, even if he was already there.

I could lie.

And I wouldn't have to "mosey home" right away, would I?

Maybe when you make a dumb new rule like this one, you deserve what you get, *Dad.* But if that's the case, why do I feel like I'm slipping even further from my goal?

At this rate, I'll *never* get my friend Kevin back!

10

THE REAL STORY

"Jack and the Beanstalk" and Me

by

EllRay Jakes

I thought this famous story was about a boy named Jack who started out doing something dumb but ended up being a hero. I thought his mom lost her job, and they ran out of food. Then Jack sold their only cow to this shady guy for some magic beans, but you can't eat magic beans. His mom got mad at him and threw the beans out the window. A huge beanstalk grew during the night, and Jack climbed to the top, probably to hide from his mom. Then Jack fought the giant who lived at the top of the beanstalk and carried home a chicken, and his mom was happy again. In fact, they ate the chicken and then lived happily ever after, and nobody made fun of Jack anymore.

That's what I thought the story was about. But I was wrong!

Here is the real story. Jack and his mom were poor, that part was true. Also, he sold the cow to the shady guy and came home with the magic beans. And his mom threw them out, and the beanstalk grew and grew.

But Jack climbed the beanstalk three times. Each time, he stole something from the giant! The first time, the giant shouted "Fee, fi, foe, fum," and Jack stole two bags of gold coins and got away. He and his mom could buy whatever they wanted, and they did.

The second time Jack climbed the beanstalk, he was just being greedy, in my opinion. He stole the giant's chicken. It turned out she could lay solid gold eggs. Score!

But even that wasn't enough for Jack, who by then was loving those magic beans. So Jack climbed the beanstalk a third time to steal the giant's gold harp that played the best music in the world. When the giant chased after him, which, P.S., who wouldn't, Jack raced back home, chopped the beanstalk down, and the giant smashed to the ground, dead. "Fee, fi, foe, FUMBLE."

Jack never got in trouble for any of this, by the way, and he and his mom lived happily ever after. Or at least until their gold ran out.

Why is this story special to me? I thought it was because Jack was a guy who messed up but turned out to be a hero. But now, all I can say is that it is special to me because it proves how you should not admire a story just because it's famous.

Also, be careful who you want to be like.

Even if I never see an actual beanstalk my whole life long, I hope I can be a hero someday. But not like Jack.

The End.

✲ 11 ✲

A CHALLENGE

WOO-HOO! So, obviously, the folk tale assignment is going just great.

Opposite.

On Monday, we worked some more on adding our personal stories to the folk tales we'd chosen. Then we turned them in to Ms. Sanchez.

That's the story you just read. I wrote it on our family room computer, so it came out pretty good. I write a lot better—and *longer*—on the computer than when I write by hand. For me, writing by hand is almost like having to carve the words on a rock.

On Tuesday, Ms. Sanchez read the stories.

First thing today, Wednesday, Ms. Sanchez gave our stories back to us with her corrections and suggestions. She told us to write them out again for homework tonight, only perfect this time.

She wrote a *lot* of stuff on my paper, by the way. I haven't read it all yet, but she said at the end of her comments that she liked it.

Oh, really, Ms. Sanchez? Even though I basically chose the wrong story?

After lunch, she is going to talk to each of us in private about our story while the other kids start making their drawings—"illustrations"—to go with their stories. I think my drawing should show Jack in jail, behind bars, for stealing the giant's gold, his special chicken, and probably some other stuff, too, but that's not how his story ended.

That tells you something about the world right there, doesn't it?

I also think the boy conferences will be short, and the girl conferences will be long. Girls seem to have a lot more to say about stuff, to make another "sweeping generalization about girls," as my dad would say.

But I'm right.

On Friday, we will read our stories aloud to the whole class. Corey will probably faint, he'll be so nervous. He's already worried about it.

Then our stories and drawings will go up on the wall, Kry predicts, because it's going to be Parents Day at Oak Glen next Tuesday. She says that's what was behind this assignment the whole time: Ms. Sanchez needed something cute to put up for Parents Day.

Right now, though, it is Wednesday nutrition break, and we are outside eating and playing at the same time, trying not to choke on our nutrition. It is one of those cool-warm mornings when the sun is shining but the wind is blowing, and everything is great.

They should make more days like this, in my opinion!

For us boys, this kind of weather is perfect for lots of things.

1. You can swing from the monkey bars, or just hang there and pretend you are an underwater deep-sea diver about to go eye-to-eye with a giant squid.
2. You can run around the playground until your

legs get numb, and you have to stop and grab your side to catch your breath. But in a good way.

3. You can play kickball, or, if the good balls are all taken, you can pretend your foot has superpowers as you kick a caved-in ball against the fence and imagine the cheering crowd.

That's what Corey and I are doing right now. "*BLAM-O!*" Corey shouts, sinking his sneaker into a crumpled, faded red kickball.

"Take *that*," I say, blasting another one with the side of my foot.

Our kickballs hit the fence with splats and drop to the pavement, and we scoop them up so we can do it again. It's not as much fun with two people as it would be if there were three, but is Kevin playing with us? *Oh, no.* He is over by the picnic tables with Jared and Stanley.

Kevin, Jared, and Stanley are crouching, almost squatting, on the concrete slab. It looks like they are either pretending to skate or pretending to be airplanes, like Alfie said to me that time.

They look kinda dumb, in my opinion—not that kicking squashy balls against a fence takes a whole lot of brains. I'm not gonna lie.

"Hey," Jared yells, catching me watching them. "Come here! I wanna tell you guys something."

"How much he hates us, probably," Corey mutters, turning his back on Jared, Stanley, and Kevin, and giving his floppy kickball another slam against the clattering chain-link fence.

"Yeah," I agree, but I take another peek at the picnic table area. Now Kevin is waving us over there, too. "Maybe we should go," I say to Corey, who is now walking around with the kickball draped over his head, arms out in front of him like he's Frankenstein. "Kevin wants us, too."

"Okay, but just wait," Corey warns, tossing off his kickball hat and catching it with one hand. "Kevin will say something mean, just so Jared will think he's so tough and everything."

"He won't," I say, picking up my kickball as we get ready for the long walk to the picnic tables. "He might just stand there and say nothing *after* Jared says something mean to us. Or Stanley does.

But I don't think Kevin has completely turned on us yet."

"Hey," Jared says when we get there.

He leaves out the "loser" this time, but I can still hear it.

"Hi, guys," Kevin says, smiling like nothing is wrong. As if he just happened to be hanging out with Jared and Stanley, not with us. He bends his knees, then jumps three inches off the concrete slab onto the grass like he's performing a skate trick on an invisible board.

"You think that's good? Watch *this*," Stanley says to Kevin, glaring at him through smudged glasses. I can tell he's mad because he's not Jared's only friend anymore. Stanley climbs up onto the picnic table bench, crouches, then springs onto the slab, arms out and legs bent, like he just landed a perfect 360-flip or something.

Virtual skating!

"Awesome," Corey says, but I can tell he's trying not to laugh—and so can Kevin, probably. Kevin shrugs and turns away.

Jared sees all this, and he scowls. He grabs my

sleeve and hauls me in close to him. "I barely even *know* Kevin and he's hanging out with me and not you," he whispers. "Loser," he finishes, pushing me away. I can smell peanut butter on his breath.

And just as the buzzer sounds, the idea comes to me. *Jared* should have chosen "Jack and the Beanstalk" for his story! It would be perfect for him, right? Jared does everything mean, just like Jack, and he never gets punished for it.

He will just go on and on until "The End."

"Friday," Jared shouts across the wind as we head for class. "After school. At the park. Skating contest. It's a challenge."

"Why don't we have a helicopter flying contest, while we're at it?" I yell back. "None of us can fly a helicopter, either!"

"Chicken," Stanley jeers, although I already showed Jared and him a long time ago that I'm *not* a chicken. And that's a story nobody can change. "Be there," Stanley shouts.

"Okay," I say, trying to picture it: Jared, Kevin, Stanley, and me, because Corey will be at swim practice, naturally. So I'll be on my own. One against three.

But—four guys at the park, pretending they can skate? Scooting down the park's bumpy paths like a bunch of babies?

What if some real skaters see us?

"Posers!" I can hear it now.

Okay. I have two days to learn at least **ONE TRICK** from Fly Reilly, the bad choice kid, I tell myself, shrugging out of my jacket when we get inside Ms. Sanchez's class. And I'm going to try, even if going over to Henry's house when Fly's there means lying to my dad.

But I'll be at that park whether I learn anything or not.

I can be at least a little gutsy, can't I? Even though I'm just EllRay Jakes, and not Jack, the gangster star of "Jack and the Beanstalk"?

12

MAKING IT YOUR OWN

"I need different blues," Annie Pat says, hunching over a drawing of herself starring as the Little Mermaid. I guess she doesn't mind the part about ending up as sea foam, or maybe she didn't read that far.

Our class moved the chairs so we are facing each other across long tables. That way, we can share the colored pencils, markers, and crayons better as we do our illustrations.

We can *supposedly* share.

"I need blue, too, for part of the Pied Piper's Hawaiian shirt," Jared argues, grabbing one of the markers. "See, I thought my guy had a lot of *pie*, and that's why all the kids followed him, but it turns out that 'pied' means 'different colors,' so—"

"Cinderella wears a blue dress under a perfectly

clean white apron," Cynthia interrupts as she corrals a few blue-colored pencils and crayons for future use. "But you guys can use these when I'm done," she adds, like she's being so generous.

"I need a light brown crayon," Emma tells Annie Pat. "Because Thumbelina slept in a walnut shell when she was a baby. That's how teensy she was." She smiles—at the thought, I guess.

"Use burnt sienna for your walnut shell, Emma," Fiona advises, reaching for a dark blue crayon to help fill in her own scary-looking night sky. She is drawing "The Little Match Girl," like she said she was going to do. Her Little Match Girl definitely looks like she has weak ankles. Fiona's illustration is fancier than anyone else's, of course.

Heather is having her conference with Ms. Sanchez right now, but before she left the table, she taped on an extra piece of paper to the bottom of her drawing so she could make Rapunzel's beautiful hair as long as she wants.

Stanley is drawing a grasshopper with a party hat on, for "The Grasshopper and the Ant." I'm not sure he read to the end of that one, either. And Corey is spending most of his time working on a cool, zigzag pattern for his tortoise's shell, because he's doing "The Tortoise and the Hare." I guess the hare has already raced past—or is busy taking the nap that makes him lose the race.

"What are you drawing, Kevin?" Corey asks, as if nothing is wrong. Like everything has been the same as usual these past couple of weeks.

We have all been **SNEAKING** peeks at Kevin's drawing. There are a lot of bloody body parts lying around, and a smiling boy is standing in the middle of them, hands on his hips.

"It's for this cool story my dad helped me find," Kevin reports after giving me a quick look. "It's called 'The Boy Who Left Home to Find Out About the Shivers.'"

"That's not even a real story," Cynthia informs him, adding some dots to the edge of Cinderella's perfectly clean white apron. Lace, probably. Cynthia would never allow even *pretend* dirt on her drawing.

"It is, too," Kevin says, not even looking at her.

"Well, *I've* never heard of it," she says, like that means anything.

Heather comes back to the table. "Your turn,

EllRay," she says to me, and so I flip my illustration facedown on the table so no one can draw a mustache or something worse on Jack, get my story, and head for Ms. Sanchez's desk.

★ ★ ★

"So, EllRay," Ms. Sanchez begins, smiling at me as I hand her my paper to look at again. "Let's talk. You wrote a lot, but I take it you were a little disappointed with 'Jack and the Beanstalk'?"

"It wasn't the way I remembered," I try to explain. "Only it was too late for me to change stories."

"That's okay," Ms. Sanchez says, pinning back some loose hair that has fallen from the shiny black bun at the back of her head. "You know, there are a couple of ways to look at this pickle you're in. First, there are a number of versions of just about every folk tale or fairy story there is, did you know that?"

"You mean people just make stuff up and change the stories?" I ask, frowning.

"Well, sure," she says, laughing. "Writers tell the stories people want and need to hear, and those needs can change over time. And some of these stories go back hundreds—even thousands—of years, so naturally they evolve."

"Huh," I say, trying to figure out what she's saying.

"Also, people *remember* the stories the way they need to," Ms. Sanchez continues. "Like you did with Jack in 'Jack and the Beanstalk,' who you said 'ended up being a hero,' with nobody making fun of him anymore."

"But when I looked on the Internet, nothing I read was the way I remembered it," I remind her. "All the versions I read said he stole stuff from the giant."

"And stealing is wrong, as you pointed out," Ms. Sanchez agrees, nodding. "But I think what those stories were really trying to say was that Jack was being clever, tricking the giant the way he did. He had to learn how to deal with someone who was mean and scary, like we all do. And remember, Jack was trying to help his mom."

"He was trespassing," I say. "*And* stealing. You can't do that just because you don't like someone, or because they're a giant. Can you?"

Maybe you can! That would be pretty cool if it were true, I think, imagining it. You could just make a list of everyone who deserves to be robbed, and—

"EllRay?" Ms. Sanchez is saying. "You wandered off."

That means I stopped paying attention for a moment, which is true.

I do that. It's one of my things.

"What I'm trying to tell you is that I'm very happy with the way you carried out the assignment,"

Ms. Sanchez says. "You did your research, then you explained how the story differed from the way you remembered it."

"But my research made a lie out of everything I liked about the story," I say.

"Not necessarily," Ms. Sanchez tells me. "What I want you to do next is to remember why the story was important to you in the first place, For example, if you were Jack, who would be the giant in your own personal story?"

Jared, I think, but I don't say anything.

"And what would your beanstalk look like?" she continues.

"What do you mean?" I ask. "Aren't they all the same? A thick, twisty vine with big leaves and stuff? Like a leaf-ladder?"

I mean, I've never actually *seen* one, but . . .

"Your beanstalk could be a symbol of something else," Ms. Sanchez tells me. "For instance, if you're afraid of the dark, 'taking a step up your beanstalk' might mean sleeping for a night without the closet light on."

And I actually know what she means for once, even though I'm not afraid of the dark. Because that's the way I was already thinking—when I decided to learn to skate so I could be friends with Kevin again, for example, or when I had to pay Alfie a nickel so she'd let me use her rug, or when I stood up to Jared when he was trying to make me look bad. Those were like steps up the beanstalk for me. Not that I'd want to have to explain that to anyone.

And caving in to Fly and deciding I might someday ignore parts of my dad's dumb new rule about Fly made me feel like I was slipping *down* the beanstalk.

"And why would you *want* to climb that beanstalk?" Ms. Sanchez continues.

To find out if I'm a **HERO** *or not*, I think, still silent. *To be friends with Kevin again.*

"Also, what would 'living happily ever after' mean to you?" she asks. "See, 'Jack and the Beanstalk' can still be your story, EllRay. It's a matter of making it your own."

"You want me to throw out what the Internet said?" I ask, surprised.

All that research? After I had to battle Alfie to use the family room computer?

"No," she says. "You should keep it in your paper,

but add a little more about yourself at the end."

Hmm.

"But are we really gonna read them out loud on Friday?" I ask, trying not to sound too horrified.

Because—what is she trying to do, make me look weak—or even cry—in front of the class?

Jared's biggest dream would come true!

Maybe Corey has the right idea, being scared about doing stuff in front of class. It can be risky.

"You don't have to make it overly personal, sweetie," Ms. Sanchez says—quietly, for once.

See, she has this bad habit sometimes of calling me "sweetie," and that means at least two days of teasing each time she does it, if anyone hears.

"You don't need to name names," she explains. Or sort of explains.

"Okay. I'll try," I tell her, hoping this will end the conversation.

"Good," she says, beaming as if our conference has been a huge success. "Now, please tell Kevin I'd like to speak to him next, okay?"

You and me both, I can't help but think.

But I just grab my paper and nod *okay.*

And I'm outta there.

13

PART OF IT

"Hi, EllWay," Alfie says from her pink bike—with training wheels we're not supposed to mention—as I plod up the driveway after school. An empty white plastic lawn chair is on the grass, and the front door is open. "I just talked to Henry's fwend," she informs me.

"Fwend" means "friend" in Alfie-speak.

"You should dress more like him," Alfie tells me, tilting her head as she inspects me. "He looks really good. He's almost a teenager, he said."

"You mean *Fly*?" I ask, scowling—because I do not want Fly Reilly talking to my little sister. He doesn't even like her! What's he up to?

Also I am frowning because I had hoped to go over to Henry's this afternoon for some serious skating practice. Maybe Henry has learned the secret to doing an ollie by now. It has to happen *some* day.

But if Fly is already over at Henry's, well, that complicates everything. I'll either have to lie to my dad and say I didn't know Fly was there, or stay home and give up my chance to learn even one small thing before the world's lamest skating contest on Friday. That's just two days away.

Alfie nods, her eyes wide. She looks like she has a secret she's dying to tell me.

"*Where* did you see him?" I ask. "And where's Mom?"

I'm kind of worried about Mom, because no way

would she leave Alfie alone outside—for more than a minute or two, anyway. Maybe not even that long.

I'll bet she didn't know Bad Choices Fly was going to come **BUZZING** by, wanting to talk to her baby girl for some mysterious reason.

"*Fly* was walking on the sidewalk," Alfie says, counting on her fingers as she explains. "*I* was riding my bike on the driveway, like now. And *Mrs.-Sandler-across-the-street* was watering her flowers and saying what a good bike rider I was. Then Mom had to go inside and put something in the oven. She said she guessed I was big enough to ride my bike alone for a couple of minutes, and I should just keep talking to Mrs. Sandler and wait for you. Only Mrs. Sandler's phone rang."

"And—I'm back. Hi, EllRay," my mom calls out, wiping her hands on a kitchen towel as she comes back outside. She tosses the striped towel onto her shoulder and sits down in the lawn chair like nothing bad just happened.

Like Fly didn't talk to Alfie.

But maybe there's still a way to rescue my afternoon—*and* warn Fly away from Alfie. Or at least try.

"Don't tell Mom about talking to Fly," I warn Alfie under my breath, and she looks at me, lips squinched shut like there's a lock on them. It's this thing we do when we're promising each other to keep quiet about something.

* * *

"Okay. Tell me what he said, Alfie," I say to my sister in a low voice half an hour later. We just finished the bean and cheese burritos our mom was keeping warm for us, and Mom has gone back to her fantasy writing.

Alfie squinches her mouth shut again and shakes her head *no*.

"That's our thing for not telling *Mom and Dad*," I remind her, but Alfie still has a sneaky look on her face.

"I can tell you part of it," she finally says. "But not the best part. That's secret."

"Okay. Tell me part of it," I say, figuring Fly couldn't have talked too long. Not if Mom was only gone a minute or two.

"Fly said he could teach me to skateboard better than you," Alfie tells me, smiling big.

"But I'm not even *trying* to teach you to skate," I say, confused.

"I know, even though I wanted you to," Alfie says, clouding up for a second. "I *mean*, he said he'd teach me to *skateboard* better than you," she tells me, drawing out the words. "Fly said he'd show me how to do this really hard trick for free, and Henry would love it, and everyone would say, 'Wow, look at that kid!' And then I'd be famous, he said. Minnie Mouse is famous," she reminds me, her voice suddenly hushed and her brown eyes wide with admiration.

Minnie is one of Alfie's old-school heroes. Alfie likes her clothes. She also likes Daisy Duck, mostly because of her long, flappy eyelashes.

"And that's not even the best part of what he said?" I ask, narrowing my eyes at Alfie the way Dad does when he's questioning me.

"Nope," she says, and she locks shut her lips again and shakes her head so hard that the tiny barrettes at the end of her puffy little braids look like they're dancing. "But I have to come with you over to Henry's."

"*No*," I say, as if that's the dumbest idea I've ever heard—which it kind of is. I'm eight, and like I said before, they can barely stand *me* going over there. Fly, anyway. Why would they want a four-year-old hanging around?

"Then you have to stay home and play horsie with me, because Mom's busy," Alfie says, a stubborn look spreading across her small, round face like it's going to stay there for a while. "Which horsie do you wanna be? Purple or two-koys?"

I guess that's supposed to be Alfie-speak for "turquoise."

"Neither one," I say. "I have homework to do."

I can *pretend* to be doing it, and then sneak out of the house, I tell myself. How hard could it be to fool a four-year-old who is chattering to a bunch of plastic horses?

Alfie eyes me as if she is reading my mind. "Let's go ask Mom," she finally says.

"But we're not supposed to bother her, remember?" I say. "Unless someone is bleeding?"

"Then we'll leave her a note about going over to Henry's house," she says, as if this is her last and best offer. "And you'll take me with you."

I stare hard at her for a second. My dad would freak if he knew I was even considering this—even if Fly wasn't there. We take extra-good care of Alfie.

"I won't bother anyone," she vows, her hand on her heart.

"Well, okay," I say, not liking it one little bit. On top of everything else, Alfie is totally getting her way—as usual. "But you have to promise not to embarrass me," I add.

"Don't embarrass *me*," Alfie says, lifting her chin.

We could keep going back and forth forever like this, so I don't say another word.

Instead, I start gathering some truly great snacks for Fly.

And then I write our note.

14

ALFIE'S BIG SECRET

"Slide! Slide your foot, fool," I can hear probably-well-dressed Fly yelling to Henry as Alfie and I walk down the Pendletons' driveway. I hear Henry's skateboard crash as it hits the ground.

"He's *stwict*," Alfie says, her voice hushed, and suddenly she is holding my hand.

"Stwict" probably means "strict" in Alfie-speak. I'm not sure about that one.

She wanted to come with me, but now she's scared? "You can always go back home," I tell her. If I'm lucky, Alfie might think it's her own idea.

"Hey, little *dude*! And little dude's little sister," Fly calls out, greeting us as though it's his house, not Henry's.

"Her name's Alfie," I say to Fly. "She wanted to come," I tell Henry in a quiet, I'm-sorry way, but Henry is busy picking himself up off the driveway and then chasing after what looks to me like a new board.

He is wearing lots of layers of clothes today, I notice—to cut down on road rash and bruises, I guess. Or to hide them from his mom.

"It's okay about Alfie," Henry finally says. "I almost did it. I almost ollied!"

"Not very *well*," Fly points out, adjusting his red-and-navy sweatshirt just so.

He is a pretty cool dresser, I have to admit. And he knows it. It's like his clothes point out what a great skater he is, too, because a bad skater would have torn pants, and rips everywhere else.

But no clothes-destroying speed wobbles or rocks in the road for Fly Reilly.

"It wasn't perfect, but almost," Henry says, mostly to me, after getting a drink from the dribbling hose coiled on the soggy patch of lawn next to the driveway's turnaround area. He wipes his mouth on his sleeve and slips me a shy, proud smile.

"You gotta remember, skating's not just a sport," Fly says, sounding important. "It's a *way of life*. So 'almost' doing something doesn't cut it, dude. You have to do it perfect. Is that food?" he asks, jumping to another subject as he nods his chin toward the bag in my hands.

"Yeah. I decided to bring some snacks," I say, shrugging like it was my own idea, not Fly's command—and hoping Mom won't notice the missing cookies, chips, and leftover burritos.

I'll deal with that when I have to. But it was for a good cause, I'll tell her—so I wouldn't get pounded by Fly Reilly, the bad choice kid.

Who I'm not even supposed to be seeing anymore.

"Next time, bring food and *money*," Fly tells me. "For plywood. Or else you can't hang with us. You gotta pay to play, little dude."

"Come *on*, Fly," Henry says, sounding just about fed up.

But Fly doesn't even notice. Instead, he points at Alfie. "She can sit over there on the stairs, and hold the food until later," he says, like it's a royal decree. "Don't eat anything," he commands her.

"Her name's *Alfie*," I say again, trying not to get mad.

I mean, I'm not exactly thrilled that Alfie made me bring her along, but she is a person. She has a name.

Fly's treating Alfie like she's just some *thing*.

"Hold Henry's old board, while you're at it," Fly tells Alfie, who has settled herself like a golden princess on the topmost step leading to the Pendletons' kitchen, the bulging bag of snacks at her side. I guess she's happy as long as she can watch her idol Henry Pendleton, because she's quiet, for once.

Very quiet.

Fly hands her Henry's old board—which is still better than my new-old board, but never mind—and hunkers down on a lower step to eyeball Henry and me.

"Now you try," Henry tells me in an encouraging way. "Just remember. Crouch, push down with your back foot, then slide your front foot to level out. That's the part I keep forgetting. And land with your knees bent. I guess you just have to mess up a few hundred times before you can get your board into the air without barely thinking about it. So you might as well get started."

"I learned much faster than that," Fly calls out, like he's arguing with Henry.

Well, maybe Fly *did* learn fast, I think, crouching on my bashed-up board. And maybe he didn't.

He doesn't exactly seem like the kind of guy who tells the truth every day of the week. Or even once a week.

My dad might be right about him.

And he's eleven years old, not eight, like me. No wonder he's a better skater!

I crouch, then move my right foot back until the board tilts up, then I try to slide my left foot forward so I can get some air and make the board come down flat, with that perfect skateboard *bang* that sounds so cool.

Instead, *I* come down flat—on the driveway.

"Here, look," Henry says as he helps me up. And he steps onto his new board to show me what he's learned.

"No, *you* guys look," Fly calls out in a funny voice, and Henry and I turn our heads toward the tile steps in what feels like **SLOW MOTION**. It's like we know we're going to see something bad.

Okay.

Fly is holding my little sister's hand to balance her. She is teetering at a weird angle on the Pendletons' top step—on Henry's old board.

This means she is pointing downhill, of course. *Seriously* downhill.

So this was Alfie's big secret!

On her head, she is wearing her bike helmet. I didn't even see Alfie bring it with her.

On her face—her *perfect* face, without even a scratch on it—I can see different feelings battling for first place.

Happiness, because she has totally surprised me.

Excitement at the idea of skating better than me, like Fly said he'd teach her to do.

Fear, because she suddenly realizes where she is, and what's about to happen.

My ears are buzzing, I'm so scared for her.

I can't figure out the expression on Fly's face at all. He looks kind of—blank.

Like I said before, what is his *problem*?

"It's 'sink or swim,' see," Fly pretend-explains to Henry and me. "If she falls, so be it. If she doesn't, by the time she gets to the bottom she'll be a skater."

"She's only four!" I yell.

"Let go, kid," Fly shouts at Alfie, who is clutching at him now with both hands. It looks like she's about to jump into his arms.

"EllWay! Help!" Alfie cries, and then Fly untangles her hands from his. And he gives her a shove down the tile stairs—on Henry's old board—in almost the very same movement.

But I am already **FLYING** through the air.

I'm almost there, Alfie.

I hurl myself onto the driveway and skid the rest of the way to break her fall.

15

GIANT

"*Waah!*" I hear Alfie cry as she bounces off me and the board skitters on its back across the turnaround toward Henry, as if he was calling it home.

But the cry is Alfie's scared-mad "What just happened?" wail, not the "I'm hurt!" one.

I am hurt, I realize, lying facedown on the cement. I did not come to Henry's today prepared to be a stuntman—or even to do any serious tricks. I was just going to try to get an inch closer to doing an ollie. So I was wearing the opposite of the clothes needed for a driveway skid.

My cheek and arms feel hot and wet, and they're starting to sting, and my knee hurts.

I feel something patter onto my back, and I lift my head to see coins bounce to the ground. Three nickels and a dime. "There you go, girl," Fly's voice says from somewhere to the right of me.

"Her name's Alfie," I mumble into the cement.

There's blood in my mouth. I must have bitten my lip or my cheek.

Yeah, Fly has a problem. But I no longer care what Fly's problem is.

"You said you'd give me a *quarter* if I did what you said," Alfie yells between gulping sobs. "You big liar!"

"What a dope," Fly says, but even he is starting to sound a little nervous. "Little dude's little sister can't even count money yet," he tells Henry.

"Dude, she's four!" Henry shouts back.

Fly tried to hurt my sister! Why? Because she peeked at him? Because she got on his nerves? Because he was *bored*?

"It's not my fault she slammed," Fly objects, which is a lie if I ever heard one, because this was *totally* his fault. "And don't 'dude' me, poser," he continues, trying to turn Henry's anger around like a 180-kickflip. "You guys are *both* a couple of posers, in fact. I don't know why I ever bothered—"

But he doesn't get the chance to finish his sentence, because I'm up—and on him.

"*Raahhh!*" I bellow, hoping that this noise, plus

the surprise of my attack, will make up for what I lack in size and strength.

I manage to knock him over, at least—like a small lumberjack cutting down a very tall tree.

As I said before, Fly is halfway between me and Henry in height—*and* he's three years older than I am, *and* his scrapes, bad choices, and general troubled kid-ness means that I'm **DOOMED**.

But I don't care.

He tried to hurt Alfie. And I'm the one who brought her over here.

"You're the poser," I yell, starting to pound his shoulder with what passes for my fist. "You're posing as a human being!"

I feel like an ant trying to battle a tarantula.

My surprise advantage has been over for about ten seconds, and Fly realizes it. He looks like he's getting ready to enjoy himself.

Fly looms over me like a giant, smiling at last. His right arm goes back for a major punch, so I duck my head and wrap myself around him like I'm made out of the strongest glue in the world, and I start to roll with him—toward the muddy patch of lawn.

"EllWay!" I hear Alfie crying from what seems like far away.

"Get off him before he hurts you, EllRay," Henry shouts, running over to us. And, to Fly, "Dude, get a grip—you're twice his size!"

"I—don't—care," Fly yells, trying his best to get far enough away from me to hit me. But I hang on tight.

And I keep rolling us toward the mud.

"If you get blood on my clothes you are going to be so sorry," Fly mutters in my ear, almost growling.

"Then I'll get blood *all—over—them*," I say, panting out the words. "And your clothes will be wrecked, and then everyone will know what a coward you are!"

This makes absolutely no sense at all, because clothes can't talk. But I'm glad I said it.

He *is* a coward. Not for fighting me, but for putting Alfie in danger.

And—Fly and I are on the lawn.

The **MUDDY** lawn, where the hose has been dribbling the whole time Alfie and I have been here today.

And what a great idea coming over here was, I congratulate myself, managing some inner sarcasm as I grind a fist into where I guess Fly's ribs might be.

"Dude! *Mud!*" Fly cries when he realizes where we are. He tries to lift his body—*our* bodies—off the ground, like he thinks maybe he can float in the air if he just tries hard enough.

He's trying to keep his stupid clothes clean! My little sister can go shooting down a flight of tile stairs face-first, for all he cares, but Fly Reilly wants to keep his clothes clean.

This guy is seriously messed up.

"Not so fly now, huh?" I say, **SMOOSHING** his perfect red-and-navy sweatshirt back and forth in the mud as I thrash the two of us around really good.

"But I'm supposed to go out to dinner with my aunties," he shouts, like I care. "And this sweatshirt is new!"

"Not anymore, it's not," I somehow manage to say, and I scoop up a handful of the mud and plant it smack on his face.

"Okay, that's *it*," Fly yells through the mud, and he reaches for my neck with both hands. "You're gonna be sorry, kid. Because I'm gonna—"

"Fly Reilly and EllRay Jakes," a grown-up's voice calls out.

An *angry* grown-up's voice.

It's about time!

✲ 16 ✲

JUST AN ORDINARY AFTERNOON

It's Henry's mom, Mrs. Pendleton—and she looks as if she can't believe what has been happening in her own backyard.

Believe it, Mrs. Pendleton.

"What in the world is going on out here?" she asks, marching down the tile steps as if that's what they were invented for. "I leave you kids alone for a *few minutes*, to make some cookies, and what happens?"

"What kind of cookies?" Fly asks from the mud, actually interested.

"He played a bad twick on me," Alfie says, still lying on the driveway and starting to cry again. "But EllWay saved me."

"Twick" means "trick," I guess.

"Alfie! Sweetheart," Mrs. Pendleton says, seeing her for the first time. She rushes to my little sister's side and scoops her into her arms. "I didn't know you were here." She smoothes Alfie's hair back, inspects her tear-streaked face, then clutches her close once more.

"She's lying," Fly calls out from the mud, shaking me off now like a flea or a mosquito, something that bothered him for a while, but no biggie.

He looks like a wreck, though, I'm happy to report.

In fact, he looks **TERRIBLE**.

"Don't call Alfie a liar, Fly," Henry says, his voice hard. "You could have knocked her teeth out, dude. Or broken one of her bones. Fly sent Alfie shooting straight down those stairs, Mom. On a *board*."

And Alfie looks up at Henry with shining eyes, of course.

Oh, great, I can't help but think. This was all the encouragement she needed.

"Then you're a liar, too, *Henry*," Fly says, trying for some of his old swagger. "You're all against me—for no reason! *I'm going home*."

And he stalks over to his skateboard like it's a loyal horse that has been waiting for him all this time.

"You're not going anywhere until I say so," Mrs.

Pendleton tells Fly, giving him the same stink-eye he's given me more than once. "But I *am* calling your mother, Fly. She can leave work early, if necessary, and come pick you up. For now, you go inside and take a shower, young man. In the downstairs bathroom. A *one towel* shower."

She's so mad that I think I'd just shake myself dry, if I was the kid she was talking to.

"And then what am I supposed to wear?" Fly asks, his hands actually on his hips, he's so mad at everyone.

Him! Mad!

"I'll see if I can find some old clothes for you to throw on," Mrs. Pendleton says.

"*Old clothes*?" Fly asks, like he can't believe what he just heard.

"And they're getting older every second you keep standing here," Mrs. Pendleton says. "Now, scoot."

And Fly scoots.

"Are you okay, EllRay?" Mrs. Pendleton asks, hurrying over where I'm standing ankle-deep in mud.

"I'm fine," I say, but my throat is actually starting to feel a little achy from where Fly almost choked me. Just the idea of it is enough to hurt, I guess.

Or maybe my throat is aching because I'm trying not to cry.

Now, of all times! When everything is okay!

But Alfie could have really been hurt. The thought of it is catching up with me again.

"EllRay! Your poor arms, and your chin! You're

bleeding," Mrs. Pendleton says, and a hand goes straight to her chest, which is something moms do when they're horrified by some kid emergency. "You need first aid. What in the *world*?" she says again.

"I—I sort of skidded when I fell," I tell her. "But I don't think I need any first aid. Anyway, my mom's a pretty good patcher-upper."

"Well, if you're sure," Mrs. Pendleton says, then she turns to Henry, as if this is all his fault.

"Henry didn't do anything wrong, Mrs. Pendleton. I promise," I say. "He was just trying to teach me how to ollie."

"He did stuff *right*," Henry's biggest fan chimes in, beaming up at him.

Poor Henry.

"Well, I guess we'd better go home," I tell Mrs. Pendleton, like this has been just an ordinary afternoon, but now we have to leave.

I don't even want to *think* about what's going to happen when Mom sees us—much less what will happen when Dad gets home.

I am in so much trouble.

"You tell your mama how sorry I am about all this," Mrs. Pendleton says. "Tell her I'll be calling as soon as I get *that* one sorted out," she adds, glancing toward the house, where I guess Fly is in the middle of his one towel shower.

"Okay. I'll tell her," I say.

When I can get a word in edgewise, that is.

17

BRAVE

"Thank you, Cynthia, for reading us your paper about 'Cinderella,'" Ms. Sanchez says on Friday afternoon. "I'm sure we all agree with you about how important it is that a person's shoes fit well, especially if they're glass slippers," she continues. "And we will keep our fingers crossed that your own handsome prince will find you some day, and that then, you'll be richer than anyone else in this room, if that's truly your wish."

"It is truly my wish," Cynthia says, and there's a serious expression on her face as she and Heather nod their heads, so I guess she means it.

I feel sorry for the prince.

Corey went first. I think Ms. Sanchez took pity on him so he could get it over with. He was so pale when he read his paper on "The Tortoise and the

Hare" that you could count every freckle on his face, but he made it through without fainting.

Reading in front of the class can be very scary for some kids, but it's only medium-scary for me. I worry that I'll get an embarrassing word to read aloud, like *abreast*, which really means side by side, or *ass*, meaning donkey. I also worry that I'll get a word I don't know how to pronounce.

But when I'm reading something *I* wrote, I know all the words. So I'm good.

I missed school yesterday, by the way, because Mom said I had to get my scrapes and bruises checked out by the doctor. Then I was supposed to "take it easy," which is not as much fun as it sounds when you're not allowed to watch TV or DVDs or play video games, much less practice your skateboard skills—because that skateboard is **GONE**. Dad didn't say for how long. Until I'm thirty, I'm guessing. And the thought of a thirty-year-old man riding a skateboard is just *sad*, especially if he's wearing a suit and a tie.

It wasn't that my dad was mad at the *skateboard*, or even all that angry about the fight, strange as it seems. He kind of understood about the fight, once Henry and Alfie explained it to him.

Instead, Dad was mad at me for two other reasons. Big ones, he said.

1. I disobeyed him about going over to Henry's when Fly was there.
2. I brought Alfie with me without asking official, in-person permission first.

Everything bad that happened to Alfie and me was because of those two things, he explained on Wednesday night after Mom patched me up the best that she could. I went to bed that night with gauze wrapped around my arms and legs like I was a mummy, and parts of my legs were stuck to the sheet in the morning. It was *gross*.

I couldn't wait to tell Corey about it!

I guess that's what I get for sliding across a driveway like a human Zamboni.

Yesterday, Thursday, the doctor did a better bandaging job than Mom, but the "flesh-colored" bandages are not *my* flesh color, so they look patchy and weird. Also, the stuff he splashed onto my scrapes hurt. I got a tetanus shot, too. **OUCH**.

I was kind of surprised the doctor didn't give me rabies shots while he was at it, considering that it was mad dog Fly Reilly at the other end of the fight. But I didn't make that suggestion to the doctor, believe me.

So now it's Friday, and here I am, waiting for Ms. Sanchez to call on me to read aloud about "Jack and the Beanstalk." When she does, everyone can stare at me as much as they want—for a few minutes, at least.

There are two rumors that have been bouncing around Oak Glen Primary School all day, ever since the kids saw my banged-up, bandaged self. The boring one, the truth I told Corey, is that I got hurt saving my little sister, then I got into a fight with the guy who tried to hurt her—even though it was more rolling in the mud than fighting. The girls like that rumor. The other rumor, the one *I* like best, is that these are skating injuries—that I had to bail in the middle of either an airwalk grab or a 50-50 grind, and I paid the price.

Yeah, *that's* what happened!

And that's why I can't take part in the skating

contest after school today, even though I'll make a special guest appearance. Maybe they'll make me the judge, since I'm supposedly such a pro.

Watch out, Tony Hawk!

"Kevin McKinley," Ms. Sanchez says, announcing the next person to read. A few kids wriggle in their seats, maybe because of his gory drawing—and because he chose a story none of us knows. Except Jared, probably. Kevin's new best friend.

If Kevin and I had been better friends lately, I could have asked him about the story. But *no-o-o.*

"All right," Kevin says, striding to the front of the class. His brown skin looks sharp next to the yellow shirt he's wearing. New, I think.

He clears his throat before starting to talk, of course.

"My story is called 'The Boy Who Left Home to Find Out About the Shivers,'" Kevin begins. "But its other name is 'The Boy Who Wanted to Learn What Fear Was.' It's real old. It's about this boy who was never afraid," he tells us. "So he got bored, because he wanted to learn what it was like to be scared. Someone pretended to be a ghost, but the boy wasn't scared at all. He pushed the pretend ghost down the stairs. After that, the boy had to leave home—and leave his father and brother, too. Sometimes heroes have to do that. And then he had a bunch of scary adventures.

"Badder and badder things happened to him," Kevin continues. "Some of the things are too bad to talk about in front of girls. But the boy kept complaining that nothing scared him. Finally, the boy decided to spend three nights in a haunted castle. If he did that, he would get all the treasure there and also marry the king's pretty daughter whether he wanted to or not. But he stayed there anyway.

"The boy had some really extreme adventures in the castle, but still nothing scared him, and he was bored even when some heads and legs fell down the chimney the second night! It was no big deal for him. That's what my drawing is about," he tells us, holding it up for inspection.

By now, most of the girls and a couple of the boys—including me—are looking nervous about where this story is going. But Ms. Sanchez seems okay, I'm relieved to see, and she's read it before.

"The last night in the haunted castle," Kevin says, "there was even a coffin in the boy's room, and the dead body tried to strangle him! But *still* he wasn't scared.

"So the boy got all the treasure, which was cool, but he also had to marry the king's daughter, even though they were way too young. But that's when he learned about the shivers, because his new wife got so tired of him complaining all the time about being bored that she threw ice water on him one night when he was asleep. But he never did learn what fear was. And the lesson is, don't get married too soon."

Kevin clears his throat again before reading the last part of his story, the personal part. "Here is why this story is special to me," he says, sneaking me a look. "A lot of stuff scares people now, like war, or bombs, or terrorists, or being poor, or getting beat up, or even worse. That stuff scares me, too, so I'm not like the boy in the story who was scared of nothing. Also, I don't get bored very often.

"But I decided I needed to have a few scary adventures, the same way that boy did. I wanted to keep my regular friends, but also hang with some new people, too. I wanted to try stuff even if it freaked me out. Because I think that's how guys learn to be brave these days, since we're not allowed to spend three nights in haunted castles. The End."

★ ★ ★

Oh, I think, watching Kevin walk back to his seat, eyes down. Why didn't he just say so? He could have told me what he was up to. I wouldn't have liked it, because—*Jared*? And Kevin might never be friends again with Corey and me the same as before. But I would have felt a whole lot better if I'd known.

I even *get* it, kind of. Maybe Kevin is scared of skating, even though his cousin is good at it, so he jumped at the chance to try something shivery and new. And he has *always* been a little scared of Jared and Stanley. Especially Jared.

Maybe Jared was Kevin's version of the beanstalk.

Cynthia's hand shoots up in the air. "What is the *point* of that story?" she asks before Ms. Sanchez even calls on her. "Because I don't think the point is that you should never get married. That bad boy never learned any lessons, and he got all the money—*and* the beautiful princess. He didn't deserve her! I don't blame her for dumping ice water all over him."

"Ideas? Anyone?" Ms. Sanchez asks the class. She sounds tired.

To my surprise, my hand goes up. And I hardly ever raise my hand in class.

"Yes, EllRay?" Ms. Sanchez says, an encouraging look on her face.

"The point of Kevin's story is that it was important to *him*. And that is a good enough reason for him to choose it," I tell Cynthia—and the whole class, even Kevin, to let him know that I understand what happened with us. A little, anyway.

"Good answer," Ms. Sanchez says, smiling big. "As I told EllRay in our private conference, girls and boys, it's a matter of making each story your own."

"You never said that to *me*," Cynthia mutters, her arms folded across her chest, and Heather nods, frowning.

"Maybe I never got the chance to say very much at all," Ms. Sanchez tells her, lifting her eyebrows but still smiling. "Now, EllRay Jakes. It's time for you to tell us about 'Jack and the Beanstalk,' and how you made *that* story your own."

My heart starts **POUNDING**. But I've already learned that I can be at least *kind of* a hero, I tell myself, clutching my paper in a death-grip as I walk stiffly to the front of the class, my knee aching and my scrapes hot and stinging underneath their bandages.

I read that same paper I'd written earlier, about how Jack stole a bunch of stuff from the giant, who finally—thanks to Jack—fell off the beanstalk and died. But I changed the ending. Here's the new one.

"Why is this story special to me? I decided I still like it, even though Jack turned into a robber. Stories don't always turn out the way you thought. But if you leave out Jack's life of crime, you still have the beanstalk, and that's cool. Also Ms. Sanchez told me there can be lots of beanstalks a kid has to climb in his life. Or her life. Sometimes you don't even know it, but when you make yourself do something scary or hard, you may be climbing one.

"The thing I learned for myself is that there can be lots of different giants to battle in your life, too, even if you're a kid! And the worst giant might not be the guy you thought it was going to be. Giants can sneak up on you, so you have to keep your eyes open. The End."

18

FREEDOM

By the time the end-of-school buzzer sounds, I feel like I know *way* too much about the kids in my class from the papers they read. My head is bursting. For instance:

1. I know that Corey likes being a fast swimmer the way the hare is a fast runner in "The Tortoise and the Hare," but his parents want Corey to be a swimming champion more than he does.
2. I know that Annie Pat Masterson was sorry she chose "The Little Mermaid" as her story, once she read all the sad and foamy details, but she still wants to be a fish scientist when she grows up. Not a mermaid scientist, though.
3. I know that Jared chose "The Pied Piper" not only so kids would follow him around, but also because he

wants to be a kid with lots of friends. He didn't say it in those exact words, but you could tell.

4. I know a lot more about Kevin, too, and why he did what he did.

I think even *Ms. Sanchez* is glad class is over for the week. Maybe she knows too much about us now, too! I hope that next week, we'll go back to plain old spelling tests and times tables instead of having to blab about "why this story is special to me."

"Move it, EllRay," Stanley says in the cloakroom as we grab all the stuff we're supposed to take home for the weekend. "Go climb a beanstalk or something."

"*You* go climb a beanstalk," Emma McGraw says, jumping to my defense. She does that sometimes, even though I wish she wouldn't. "And leave EllRay alone, Stanley. He got hurt being brave. Being a ***HERO***. Are you going to the skating contest at the park anyway?" she asks, turning to me.

"Yeah. I'll stop by for a couple of minutes, I guess," I tell her.

Technically, I'm supposed to go straight home

from school, but the park is on the way home, isn't it? And I won't have any fun, so it should be okay.

"But *you* aren't going, are you?" I ask Emma. "You and Annie Pat don't even skate."

"Not yet. But Kry does," she tells me. "And we want to watch. It's *Friday*," she adds, like that explains everything.

And in a way, it does. Friday has its own special personality, I think, especially on a day like today when the sun is shining, the wind is blowing, the clouds are bouncing around the sky, and everything outside smells good. That's because it's April, my mom says, and April means spring. But who cares what month it is?

It just feels good to be outside!

Corey has already been picked up by his mom for swim practice. But in the playground, kids with bikes and skateboards are racing over to the pen, where the custodian is standing near the open gate like a sentry. The third grade kids, especially, are eager to grab their boards and take off for Eustace B. Pennypacker Memorial Park.

It's a terrible park—just grass, trees, and a couple of benches for old people to sit on and do whatever it is they do. And it's really small. Us kids hardly ever go there.

But it's nearby, and there are some paths we can skate on. Or at least scoot on.

Other kids can, I mean. Not me.

I limp down Oak Glen's wide front steps and wave good-bye to the principal. He's always there to see us off on Fridays. Corey says the principal just wants to make sure we're really leaving.

And suddenly, I remember the exact way I felt one week ago today, how I wanted to know the secret feeling those other kids had as they picked up their skateboards from the pen at the end of the day.

I wanted *freedom.*

But on Friday afternoons, I see now, it's as if everyone in the whole school is escaping from an even bigger pen, an invisible one. And the same weekend is waiting for all of us! Anything fun could happen—even if you're a kid who is temporarily in trouble, like me.

So *I* get to have that freedom feeling, too! We all do.

I'll probably end up playing horsie with Alfie all weekend, I think, smiling anyway as I work my way through the crowd of kids toward the sidewalk leading to the park. Or I'll be forced to help her sell lemonade, so she can make enough money for that Golden Sparkle Corral she wants so much. But who cares? At least Alfie's not the one covered in bandages.

I saved her from that.

★ ★ ★

"Hey, EllRay," Jared yells when we're finally at the park. "Watch this." And arms out and legs stiff, he starts scooting his board down a sloping path. Goofy foot, of course. It's like he's surrounded by prickly cactuses, he's being so careful.

A couple of girls clap their hands, including Heather.

That should make Jared at least a little happy—as if he has some extra friends.

"Watch *this*," Stanley says, and he swoops down the same path, knees bent.

"EllRay," my old friend Kevin shouts. "Watch this!" He heads down the path, too, only he manages to swerve back and forth a little as he goes.

We *are* a bunch of posers, I think, smiling as I give him a thumbs-up. None of us is all that good at skating, not yet. But who cares? We're all having fun, even the kids like me who are only watching. And fun is what **COUNTS**.

Of course, having the right audience helps.

"Hey," someone calls out. "Watch this!" And down the sloping path comes Kry Rodriguez, her pink helmet glittering in the sun. Knees bent, swooping, shiny black hair flying behind her. And—*up* she goes. *She's on the curb.*

Kry's the first one of us who can do an ollie! But nobody hates her for it, because she's Kry.

Like I said before, I don't know how she pulls that off, being so nice.

"That was cool," Kevin says, edging up to me. "I wanna learn."

"Me, too," I admit. "But I'm grounded from skateboards for a while."

Until I'm thirty.

"Oh well," Kevin says, smiling as he shrugs.

"I liked your story about the shivers," I say, trying to sound normal, even though it feels weird to be talking to him again. "That was funny, about the ice water."

"Yeah," Kevin says. "But it's a messed-up story, especially when he has to marry that princess."

We don't mention the end part of Kevin's paper, when he told us why the story was special to him. When he talked about needing to have some adventures and hang with new people, even though he wanted to keep his old friends, too.

And Kevin doesn't mention fighting random giants or climbing any beanstalks.

We don't need to go over old stuff like that, because that was then.

And now is now.

Stuff changes. But for today, anyway, things are okay.

In fact, things are better than okay!

TURN THE PAGE TO SEE
ALL OF ELLRAY'S ADVENTURES!

EllRay Jakes may be the smallest kid in Ms. Sanchez's third-grade class, but he has a big personality! And he's not going to let Jared, the biggest kid in class, call him a chicken or get in the way of a trip to Disneyland. All EllRay has to do is stay out of trouble for one week—and keep away from Jared. The question is, can he do it?

EllRay Jakes is a Rock Star!

EllRay wishes he had something cool to brag about. Everyone else in his third-grade class does. Jared's dad owns a brand-new car with flames painted on it, and Kevin's dad is rich, but all EllRay's geologist dad has is a collection of rocks. *Boring!* Or is it? They *are* from all over the world . . . and when EllRay brings some of the rocks into school, everyone is impressed. In fact, they're so impressed, they keep them! Now EllRay needs a plan to rescue his dad's rocks . . . before his big problem lands him in *gigantic* trouble.

EllRay Jakes walks the plank!

Things are going just swimmingly for EllRay. But everything comes screeching to a halt when his younger sister accidently over-feeds the classroom goldfish EllRay was taking care of over spring vacation. Zippy is a gon-er. Fortunately, most of his classmates are sympathetic. But not bossy Cynthia. She sees this as an opportunity to blame EllRay for her own mess-ups. Must EllRay now walk the plank for stuff that he *didn't* do?

EllRay Jakes the Dragon Slayer!

EllRay knows a thing or two about getting picked on. So when he sees his sister, Alfie, being bossed around by a dragonlike girl at her school, EllRay wants to share his wisdom. As her older (and wiser!) brother he has a duty to show her that she should stand up for herself. But it's a bit more complicated than he thought. Can EllRay help Alfie figure out her own way to slay this dragon?

EllRay Jakes and the Beanstalk

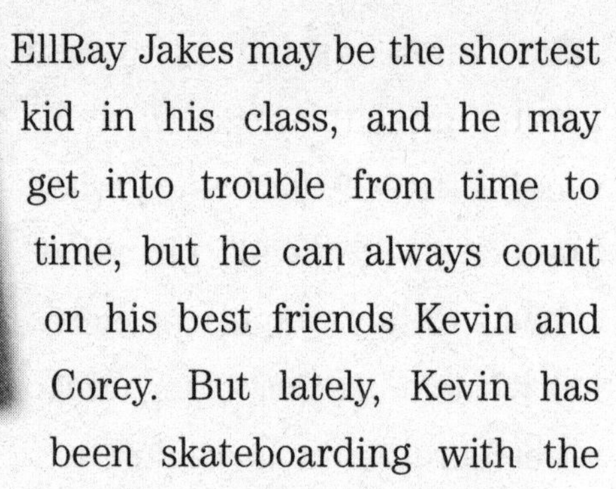

EllRay Jakes may be the shortest kid in his class, and he may get into trouble from time to time, but he can always count on his best friends Kevin and Corey. But lately, Kevin has been skateboarding with the meanest boy in class. Could EllRay be losing one of his friends?

Not giving up without a fight, EllRay asks his older neighbor to show him a few jaw-dropping skateboard moves—like ollies and kickflips. EllRay must learn as many tricks as he can before the secret boys-only third grade skate-off. But will it be enough?

EllRay Jakes is Magic!

When EllRay and his friends hear about the school talent show, they're not impressed. They're too old for that stuff. But their teacher, Mrs. Sanchez, isn't so quick to let her students off the hook. Five students absolutely *must* try out, and EllRay somehow ends up being one of them. Now he has to figure out something he's talented at . . . like maybe magic?

But the pressure's on. It's up to EllRay to take the stage and show his classmates and the whole school that he's not only talented but *magic*.